'Slow down, Jo! You're going way too fast.'

But she didn't seem to hear him. She sat gripping the steering wheel, staring almost unseeingly through the windscreen. Gordy saw the hospital loom up on their left – he was anxious now to get home, and in one piece...

Titles in the Heart Rate series

HEART RATE

stress

Charlie Hope

An imprint of HarperCollinsPublishers

First published in Great Britain by
HarperCollins*Publishers* Ltd in 1996
This edition published by Collins in 2000
Collins is an imprint of
HarperCollins*Publishers* Ltd,
77-85 Fulham Palace Road,
Hammersmith, London W6 8JB

The HarperCollins website address is
www.**fire**and**water**.com

1 3 5 7 9 10 8 6 4 2

Text copyright © Keith Miles 1996, 2000

The author asserts the moral right to be
identified as the author of the work.

ISBN 0 00 675491 0

Printed and bound in Great Britain by
Omnia Books Limited, Glasgow

Suzie, Mark, Bella, Gordy and Karlene share more than just a house. As City Hospital students, they are bonded together by its stresses and strains, emergencies and excitements, romances and rewards.

Suzie Hembrow: Student Radiographer

Tough, honest and independent, Suzie sets herself high standards and works hard. A natural organiser and listener, she often provides a helping hand or a shoulder for others to cry on – though she doesn't find it so easy to confide her own problems. Can she take the pressure of life at City Hospital?

Mark Andrews: Student Nurse

Mark has plenty of stars in his eyes about his chosen profession – not least because his favourite TV programme is *Casualty*. Shy with girls, he puts up with a lot of teasing from friends – but that doesn't stop him from falling head over heels in love at times. Utterly devoted to his duties, is he in danger of neglecting himself?

Bella Denton: Student Nurse

Lively and impulsive, life is either completely wonderful or utterly miserable for Bella. She loves being a nurse, especially when she's on the children's ward, but her volatile temper lands her in trouble with Sister Killeen on a daily basis! Bella attracts problems as easily as she attracts boyfriends – will it all end in tears?

Gordy Robbins: Medical Student

Bright, impetuous and a touch arrogant, Gordy often needs taking down a peg or two — something his friends are only too ready to do! He has a crazy sense of humour and no shortage of girlfriends, although the one he truly fancies is completely out of reach. He finds it hard to settle to the responsibilities of his student life — will it land him in trouble?

Karlene Smith: Student Physiotherapist

Dependable and supportive, Karlene has a wisdom far greater than her years. She relates well to all people and is never flustered in a crisis. She's the most even-tempered of the group and prefers to avoid conflict, although this doesn't stop her from speaking her mind if pushed. But is her warm and friendly nature in danger of being misinterpreted?

Five students: one bathroom. Every morning at City Hospital begins with a drama.

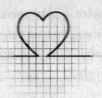

Chapter One

Gordy Robbins was in a great mood as he and Jo tumbled out of the pub. The lecture had been interesting, they'd had an excellent meal at the bar and the conversation with their friends had been very lively. They'd all enjoyed themselves that night. But little did Gordy know he'd soon come terrifyingly close to death.

Swaying slightly as they reached the car, he fumbled for his keys and then tried in vain to open the driver's door – but the key simply refused to go into the lock. Jo took over.

'I'm driving, Gordy,' she said, firmly. 'Remember? You're just a passenger tonight.'

'But I feel fine, Jo.'

'After four pints of beer you probably feel euphoric but that doesn't mean you should get behind the wheel of a car. You'd be lethal.'

Gordy seemed surprised. 'Four pints?' he said. 'Are

you sure I had that much?'

'Yes,' said Jo with a tolerant smile. 'And that was on top of the wine you had with your meal. Just be grateful I'm teetotal – I've had nothing stronger than tomato juice all night.'

'Yuk!'

'But it kept me sober, didn't it?'

Gordy nodded and handed the keys over to her before staggering round to the front passenger door. In the pub, during the cut-and-thrust of an argument with the other medical students, he had drunk too much beer, too fast. He felt queasy.

'Thank goodness you're here, Jo!'

'You always say that. Get in,' she said with a grin. 'And no singing this time. You've got a voice like a frog with a sore throat.'

'But I used to be in the school choir,' said Gordy, plaintively.

'They must have been tone deaf!'

Jo unlocked the doors and they got into Gordy's ancient Vauxhall Astra. She strapped him into his seat belt before she put on her own. She really liked Gordy and she seemed to have become his unofficial minder. It had all started at a party when some of the other students had spiked his drink. They'd thought it was funny to see Gordy staggering around in a daze, but Jo had felt sorry for him. When he'd passed out on the carpet, she had been the one who'd helped him back to his car and driven him safely home.

'What would I do without you, Jo?' he mumbled.

'Hit the first lamppost.'

'You're a friend. Know that?'

'Yes, Gordy.'

Jo's mind suddenly seemed to cloud over – it was almost as if someone had put a blindfold over her eyes. The sensation only lasted a few seconds but it scared her. She shook her head slightly, confused, and the feeling seemed to go away.

'Why aren't we moving?' complained Gordy. 'Come on, Jo. Take us back to City Hospital.'

Jo felt fine now. She was relieved as she turned on the engine.

Jo Barnes, or Joeline, as her real name was, was a slightly plump girl with expressive dimples in her cheeks and a mass of brown curly hair. Everyone liked Jo. She was friendly, cheerful and completely reliable. She was also very intelligent and Gordy often sought her help when he couldn't understand something they were studying.

They were close friends but there was no romantic interest between them. Gordy treated her as if she were a favourite sister and she looked after him in her easy and practical way. But she was glad that he'd stopped teasing her about her voice – it was the one thing that had annoyed her. She came from Birmingham and Gordy had made a point of talking about her slight Brummy accent.

Turning on the lights, she pulled away from the kerb.

'Great lecture!' Gordy said.

'Gilbert Buchanan's always worth listening to, even if we did have to drive twenty miles to hear him speak. But it's a pity he couldn't speak at City Hospital.'

'He does that all the time, Jo. This was the Annual Memorial Lecture at St Catherine's Hospital. What an amazing place! They've got a huge patient turnover. And all those new buildings and great facilities – I'd love to work there.'

'I prefer our hospital,' said Jo, thoughtfully.

'What? Even with all its faults?'

'Yes,' she said. 'I know some of the buildings are a bit old but it's got so much more atmosphere than St Catherine's. I hate those super hi-tech hospitals. They're so impersonal, they almost make you feel as though you're living somewhere in the future.'

'Well, City Hospital makes me feel we're in the age of the dinosaurs!' said Gordy with feeling.

'You're right, Gordy – and you're the missing link!'

They chatted about both hospitals for a while until Gordy started to yawn uncontrollably. After a few minutes, his head lolled forward and he went fast asleep.

Jo glanced at him indulgently. Gordy looked very

contented. His eyes were shut and he was smiling. He knew that Jo was a careful driver. He felt safe in her hands.

But Gordy was mistaken.

Thump! He was jolted out of his sleep.

Bump! Bump!

Something seemed to be hitting him. It took him a few moments to focus his eyes and realise what was happening. Jo was driving at speed through a built-up area and the car was zig-zagging crazily along the road.

Thump! They hit the kerb again. Gordy was wide-awake now.

'Slow down, Jo! You're going way too fast!'

But she didn't seem to hear him. She sat gripping the steering wheel, staring almost unseeingly through the windscreen. Gordy saw the hospital loom up on their left – he was anxious now to get home, and in one piece!

'What are you doing, Jo?' he shouted. 'Take it easy!'

There was another tearing crump as the car hit a bollard in the middle of the road.

Jo eased her foot off the accelerator and Gordy relaxed slightly but she still didn't seem to hear him. With relief, Gordy realised she was slowing down because they were approaching a fork in the road, and her face puckered with concentration as she tried to work out which way to go.

'Stop!' cried Gordy. 'Jo, just pull over and stop!'

But she ignored him. The car swung crazily off the main road as she drove down the street that forked off to the right. They began to pick up speed again. Gordy was very frightened now.

'This is a dead end, Jo! Look out!'

'What?' She seemed to hear his voice from far away.

'A cul-de-sac! There's no way out! STOP!'

As the headlights swung onto the brick wall ahead of them, Jo finally came to her senses. Jabbing her foot down hard on the brake, Jo sent the car into a long, uncontrolled skid. The noise of screeching tyres was ear-splitting and Gordy braced himself for the crash.

Jo had lost all control. The car mounted the pavement, knocked over a dustbin then screamed towards the brick wall at the end. The thud was sickening. The front bumper smashed, the headlights exploded and the bonnet jerked a foot into the air as a fountain of water shot up from the radiator.

The safety belts jammed hard into their bodies, holding them securely. Gordy was jarred but otherwise uninjured and his first thought was for Jo as he reached across to her.

'Jo! Are you OK?'

'I-I think so,' she replied, shakily.

'You nearly killed us! What were you doing?'

Jo shuddered. 'I don't know, Gordy,' she said, distantly. 'I really don't know.'

Then she burst into tears.

Chapter Two

Suzie Hembrow hadn't even expected to like them. Pop groups didn't interest her at all – though she did make an exception for Blur. But much to the disgust of her friends, she really preferred Country Music. She'd only agreed to go along to the gig because her good friend Mark Andrews had a spare ticket. They'd changed at the hospital and gone straight to the club.

But the evening had changed her mind completely – she'd had a brilliant time.

'Well?' said Mark, shouting over the noise of the applause. 'What do you think?'

'They're fantastic!' said Suzie, smiling enthusiastically.

'Well, I think so. They're a bit rough at the moment but they seem to get better every time I see them.'

'They seem very professional to me,' she said.

'Tom's worked really hard with them,' Mark explained. 'He's the vocalist. He runs the group.'

'And plays lead guitar,' noted Suzie admiringly. 'He really makes them. What's his surname?'

'Peterson, Tom Peterson.'

'He's good, Mark. He's very good.'

The audience obviously thought so. The club was packed and the applause was mixed with screams and whistles from the fans. Tom Peterson stepped up to the microphone again and played the introduction to his next song. As the sound filled the room, the crowd became silent.

The group was called Stress. There were three guitarists, a keyboard player and a drummer, but what made Stress quite unusual was that all, except Tom, were female. He was supported by four attractive girls all dressed tonight in black leather. For some numbers, they provided the vocal backing as well.

Suzie had never seen a girl on drums before but her attention was mostly taken by Tom. He had a deep, dreamy voice with a wide range – he was really talented. Tall and slim with thick black hair and blue eyes, he was wearing leather trousers and a blue shirt. Suzie couldn't take her eyes off him. She felt a pang of envy as she glanced round the rest of the group, wondering which one of them was lucky enough to be his girlfriend. Tom was so great to look at that he could probably take his pick from anyone.

Mark was whispering in her ear.

'They write all their own songs,' he was saying.

'And Tom does most of them. I think they could really be successful.'

'Have they made any records?'

'Not yet, Suzie. But I'm sure they will soon.'

'I'd buy one,' she found herself saying. Tom Peterson certainly had style; there was a sense of frenetic energy about the other members of Stress but he was very laid back. He sang the words of the song with no apparent effort and when he struck his guitar he produced a thrusting rhythm. Suzie couldn't keep still. The last number was the best and the crowd went crazy as the band reached the end.

The girls nearest the stage tried to reach up and touch Tom but he stayed tantalisingly out of reach, grinning and waving at his fans. Suzie wished she could get closer too but there was no chance of that. Stress were being mobbed.

'Fancy a drink?' suggested Mark.

'We'd never get served,' she shouted above the noise. 'Look – the place is heaving. We'd probably have to queue for hours.'

'Let's slip out the back way, Suzie. There's a bar round the corner. We can't hear ourselves speak in here.'

Suzie was reluctant to leave – the atmosphere in the club was so exciting – but she realised that she had no chance of getting anywhere near Tom. Besides, right now he was being pulled off stage by the drummer, a stunning girl with white-blonde hair. Suzie decided that she must be his girlfriend.

'OK, Mark,' she sighed. 'Let's go.'

The bar was less than fifty yards away but it seemed like a different world. Some nondescript music was playing in the background and there was none of the crush they'd experienced at the club. They could actually sit in comfort over their drinks and have a proper chat. Mark was talking enthusiastically about his latest project.

'It's all a question of building up stamina, Suzie. That's why I train every morning. I'm putting as many miles as I can into my legs. I'm not just going to run in this marathon, I'm going to finish it.'

'Good for you, Mark.' Suzie gave him an encouraging smile but she was only half-listening. While Mark described the marathon course, she was still thinking about Tom Peterson in his leather trousers. She just couldn't get him out of her mind.

'It's such a worthwhile cause,' said Mark. 'Don't you think so, Suzie?'

'Hmmm?' She came out of her reverie. 'What is?'

'This sponsored marathon.'

'Oh, yes Mark,' she agreed. 'Very worthwhile. All the money goes towards the cost of a new scanner at the hospital, doesn't it? It must give a real purpose to the race.'

'Exactly! So how much will you sponsor me for?'

She laughed. 'I knew you'd ask that!'

'Gordy's going to pay one pound a mile because he doesn't think I'll last more than a few hundred metres. He'll get a nasty shock when I finish the course and take twenty-six quid off him.'

'What are most people pledging?'

'About twenty pence a mile.'

'Well, you can put me down for that.'

'Thanks, Suzie. I'm determined we'll get that scanner.'

Mark grinned amiably and pushed his spectacles up the bridge of his nose. He was a wonderful friend and a real support in times of crisis but Suzie's mind kept drifting back to Stress. Mark couldn't compete with Tom.

Then, twenty minutes later, something extraordinary happened. They were discussing their plans for the next day at the hospital, when a tall figure came into the bar. He was wearing a long dark coat and an old hat pulled down over his eyes, but Suzie thought there was something familiar about him. It was the way he moved. As he went across to the bar to get himself a drink, she caught a glimpse of his face.

It was him. It was Tom – she was certain of it.

On impulse, she did something that later she couldn't believe she'd done. She got up and went over to him.

'Stress were fantastic tonight,' she said, smiling at him.

'Oh – yeah, thanks.' He looked very defensive.

'Look, I'm not going to bother you or anything. I mean, I don't often go to gigs like this but... well, I did tonight and I thought you were great!'

'Thanks,' he said again.

'I just wanted to tell you...' she ended lamely, feeling very embarrassed now.

Tom Peterson gave her a dazzling smile and nodded.

Suzie turned away. 'Look, sorry, I won't bother you any more...'

'No, that's OK,' he said, touching her arm to detain her and, she had to admit to herself later, sending a shiver of pleasure right through her. 'Let me buy you a drink or something.'

'A drink?' Suzie was stunned.

'Isn't that why people come into a bar?' he teased.

'Yes, oh, y-yes,' she stammered.

'So what will it be... er...?'

'Suzie. My name's Suzie Hembrow.'

'I'm Tom. What would you like, Suzie?'

She felt rather weak. 'Well, anything,' she murmured. 'Anything at all would be fine – thanks.'

'Are you sure neither of you is injured?' asked Bella Denton.

'Yes, quite sure,' insisted Gordy.

'You should have been checked out in Casualty.'

'I suggested that, but Jo refused to go.'

'So what did you do?' asked Karlene Smith.

'I walked her home and then came straight back here.'

'But what about your car?'

'I had to abandon that,' he said. 'I dread going back in the daylight to see the full damage. It was a nightmare. Jo drove straight at the brick wall. Anybody watching would have thought we'd made a suicide pact!'

Gordy was back now in the calm and safety of the house he shared with Bella, Karlene, Suzie and Mark. But he still felt very shocked by his experience with Jo and quite mystified as to why it should have happened.

'Jo!' he said. 'Of all people!'

'That's what I was thinking,' observed Bella. 'She's about the only sane person in your group at medical school. Jo holds you all together, she's so dependable.'

'Not any more, Bel.'

'Had she been drinking?'

'Only tomato juice.'

'What about drugs?' asked Karlene.

'Not in a million years!'

'So what made her freak out?'

'Who knows, Kar? She certainly doesn't. When she saw what a narrow escape we'd had, she was as scared as I was. And she was driving in such a crazy way before that – bumping into the kerb and hitting bollards in the middle of the road. Jo's driven me home loads of times. She knows the way inside out. So why take a wrong turning?'

'What did she say about that?'

'She just said "I forgot, Gordy, I forgot." I'll tell you something, next time I need a lift home, I certainly won't ask Jo!'

'That's a horrible attitude!' Karlene said, surprised.

'Yes,' agreed Bella, 'you should feel sorry for her, Gordy, not angry.'

'Sorry!' he cried. 'How can I feel sorry for someone who nearly sent me to an early grave?'

'It was an accident,' said Karlene. 'And Jo was just as much at risk as you. Stop thinking of yourself, Gordy. This must have happened because there's something wrong with poor Jo. As a medical student, you should try and find out what it is. And as a friend, you should be very sympathetic.'

'Think how terrible she must be feeling,' said Bella. 'Stop being so selfish.'

'Is wanting to stay alive being selfish?' he asked.

'You know what I mean,' said Karlene. 'Stop seeing it entirely from your own point of view. Put yourself in her place. She must be feeling really guilty.'

Gordy suddenly felt very tired and worried. His friends were right. He should be thinking about Jo.

She was usually the most cautious driver in the whole medical school and now she'd driven them both straight into a brick wall. There must be something seriously wrong with his friend to make her crack up like that.

'One consolation, anyway,' said Bella.

'What's that?' he asked.

'The damage will be covered by your insurance.'

'No it won't, Bel.'

'Aren't you insured?' she asked, horrified.

'I am – but Jo isn't. Not for driving my car, anyway.' He sighed. 'I just hope one of those witnesses in the cul-de-sac doesn't report the accident to the police or they'll start asking awkward questions. The crash was so loud we brought everyone in the neighbourhood out. And they weren't too pleased with us, either.'

'Forget them,' advised Karlene. 'You're both safe and sound, that's the important thing.'

Just then, they heard the front door opening – it was Mark.

'How was the gig at the club?' asked Bella.

'Great!' he said.

'I thought Suzie went with you.'

'She did, Bella. But she won't be back just yet. We went to hear Stress and Suzie met the lead singer, Tom Peterson, when we went for a drink. He started chatting to her and that was that. No point in me hanging around, really.'

'You mean, Suzie just ignored you?' asked Karlene.

'No, not exactly,' explained Mark. 'She seemed to forget I was there. Tom made a real impression on her and Suzie just couldn't take her eyes off him. She's really fallen for him — I've never seen her like this before.'

Chapter Three

Tom Peterson was even more good-looking face to face. Mark had been right, Suzie couldn't take her eyes off him. They sat in a quiet corner of the bar with their drinks. There was no sign of the self-confident, up-front performer that Tom was on stage. He seemed sensitive and spoke quietly – Suzie couldn't believe it was the same person.

'I thought you'd still be at the club,' she said.

'Being pursued by the fans? No thanks! I put on my disguise and sneaked across here for a quiet drink. If I was still at the club, the kids would be banging on the dressing-room door demanding my autograph. I hate all that stuff.'

'I hope you don't think I was following you – do you?'

'This is different, Suzie. I wanted to buy you a drink and have a chat, remember? I can tell you're not a screaming kid. You're more mature and I can see you've got a serious side.'

'Is that good or bad?' asked Suzie, smiling at him.

'It's good. Very good.'

'That's a relief.'

'I feel I can be myself with you.' He took his hat off and put it on the table. 'I don't have to play a part.'

Now Suzie could see him properly for the first time. He was gorgeous. For a moment, she was completely tongue-tied. She couldn't believe her luck. If they could see her now, the other fans of Stress would be green with envy.

'Do you really like our band?' he said.

'Yes, I thought you were great. Do you write all your own music?'

'Yeah and the lyrics as well. What other groups do you like?'

'Well, Blur and—'

'Who else?'

'Nobody, really,' she admitted. 'The truth is, I'm not into pop music, really. I prefer Country Music.'

'There's nothing wrong with that. I like it myself.'

'Do you?' she asked, surprised.

'Yeah. Garth Brooks is one of my favourites.'

'And mine!' she said, pleased they had something in common.

'I was afraid you'd sneer at me, Tom. My friends certainly do. They think that Country Music is some sort of joke. They're always having a go at me about it.'

'I should ignore them, if I were you,' said Tom.

He sipped his drink and looked at her with interest. Suzie didn't look, dress or talk like the girls he usually met. She was different: bright and attractive with an air of independence about her. Tom thought her freckles were cute, too.

'I'm flattered,' he said. 'Flattered that you think Stress are worth coming to listen to. We must do something right if we can tempt you to come along to a gig. What made you decide to come tonight, Suzie?'

'It was my friend Mark. He had a spare ticket. He's a big fan of yours.'

'Is he your boyfriend?'

'No, no,' she said, quickly. 'Nothing like that. We share a house with three other students from the hospital. I'm a trainee radiographer.' She saw his smile broaden. 'What's funny?'

'I'm glad you and this Mark aren't an item, that's all.'

'No chance of that. In fact—'

Suzie broke off. It suddenly dawned on her that she'd forgotten all about Mark. She was so occupied with Tom that everything else had gone out of her head. She'd turned her back on the very person who'd introduced her to Stress. Guiltily, she leapt to her feet and looked across the room.

'He's gone!' she exclaimed. 'Mark isn't here anymore.'

'Maybe he decided to go home.'

'I left him at that table over there.'

'He probably got tired of waiting, that's all.'

'I must find him and apologise.'

'Later,' he said, getting up from his chair.

'But he'll be really angry with me, Tom, I ought to go.'

'Give him time to cool off. Go and find him later,' he repeated, taking her by the arm. 'I don't want you to disappear now, just as we're having a chat. Relax. And don't worry about getting home, I'll drive you.' He grinned. 'OK?'

'All right,' she agreed. 'Yes, thanks, Tom, that would be great.'

When the two girls had gone to bed, Mark and Gordy stayed up to chat over a cup of coffee. Mark was amazed to hear about Gordy's car crash and his training as a student nurse took over as he leant across to him.

'Are you suffering any after-effects?' he asked.

'Yes!' wailed Gordy. 'I'm shaking like a leaf.'

'Yes, Gordy, but any aches and pains?'

'Yes, all over.'

'Any other signs?'

'Sheer panic whenever I remember what happened.'

'You're in shock, Gordy.'

'I was very nearly killed!'

'Exactly. A severe shock to your system. You need time to rest and recover. So does Jo,' continued Mark. 'It must have been catastrophic for her when she realised what she'd done. She was lucky she braked when she did.'

'She only did that because I was yelling at her.'

'Yes, Gordy. But supposing she'd been in the car on her own, with no passenger to alert her. She would have had a head-on collision with that brick wall.' Something bothered him. 'Are you sure you didn't distract her in some way?'

'Quite sure.'

'You do go a bit mad when you've had a few beers. If you'd taken Jo's attention off the road…'

'But I didn't, Marco. I was fast asleep until she started bouncing the Astra off the kerb. You're as bad as Bel. She accused me of trying to kiss Jo while she was driving. As if the accident was my fault!'

'Well, something must have distracted her. Did you say something to upset her?'

'No! Look, please don't keep on about it. I've told you the truth so let's leave it at that.'

'OK. Sorry.'

'I want to put it all behind me. All right?' Gordy checked his watch and started to look restive. 'It's almost midnight. Suze should've been back ages ago.'

'She'll be home soon.'

'Who is the guy, anyway?'

'Tom Peterson. He's the vocalist with a group called Stress.'

Gordy looked stunned. 'And you left him alone with Suzie?'

'She can look after herself.'

'But she went with you, Mark. You shouldn't have left her on her own. Suze might be in danger. You know what the pop world's like – drugs, booze, sex.'

'Not this group. Stress are squeaky clean.'

Gordy looked sceptical. 'With all those temptations? You should have stayed with Suze to protect her.'

'From what? Tom's got hundreds of girls to choose from at the club. If that's what he was after, why did he come to the bar? He obviously wanted to avoid them. He had no idea we'd be in there,' argued Mark. 'Don't get so worked up, Gordy. Let's be honest, you're not really interested in her safety, are you? You're just jealous!'

'No I am not!'

'You fancy Suzie like mad, don't you?' Mark went on.

'I'm very fond of her, that's all. And I don't want her being chatted up by some drug-crazed musician.' He glanced at his watch again. 'Where on earth is she?'

On cue, they heard a vehicle draw up outside the house.

'I bet that's her now,' said Mark.

Gordy dived to the window and pulled back the

curtain. A battered old van stood throbbing at the kerb close to the lamppost. Emblazoned across it in large letters was the name S T R E S S with graffiti all round it. Gordy was shocked.

'He's probably got Suze trapped inside there.'

'Yeah, yeah,' said Mark with a grin. 'Look out for the teeth marks on her neck when she comes in.'

Suzie and Tom sat in the van – not speaking. They were just enjoying being together. Time had flown since they'd met in the bar and Suzie and Tom had been busy finding out about each other. They might have stayed sitting silently in the car together indefinitely if a sudden downpour hadn't jerked them out of their companionable silence. Rain began to drum hard on the top of the van and cascade down the windscreen. Tom sat forward. He was thoughtful.

'Do you think I was right to drop out of college?' he asked her now.

'Only you can answer that, Tom.'

'I didn't really give it a chance. I was only there two weeks.'

'And you walked out to form a pop group?'

'Yeah, I must've been mad. But I just couldn't hack the idea of three years studying Industrial Design.'

'Well then, it sounds as though you were right to drop out,' she decided.

'I just worry that Stress might fail.'

'You can go back to college – start again.'

He grinned at her. 'Maybe I'll switch to radiography.'

'There's stress of a different kind in that,' said Suzie.

They laughed. Suzie was so glad that she'd acted on impulse at the bar. Tom was great. He was genuinely interested in her work and very honest about the problems in his own career.

The rain became heavier and the van began to echo with the force of the storm. Suzie was suddenly conscious of the time.

'It's late,' she said. 'I must go in. I have to be up at seven tomorrow.'

'Seven!' Tom looked horrified.

'Six-thirty if I want to get in the bathroom first!'

'The earliest I ever wake up is eleven.'

'I've done three hours' work at the hospital by then!' said Suzie and they grinned at each other again.

There was a long pause. Suzie was reluctant to leave Tom and the intimacy of the van.

'Well,' she said at last, 'thanks for the lift, Tom.'

'My pleasure,' he said.

'And good luck with your group!'

'I'll need it.'

'Right. I'd better be off, then.'

'Will I see you again?'

'Probably,' she said. 'Next time Stress have a gig in

the area, I'll definitely be out there in the crowd.'

'I'd rather see you on your own, Suzie.'

Her heart began to pound. 'Well…'

'Give me your number and I'll phone you, OK?'

'Right,' she said, fumbling in her handbag for a slip of paper and a pen. She scribbled the number in the half-dark and handed the paper to Tom. 'Evenings are the best time to get me.'

'I'm usually wide-awake by then.'

They laughed again. Tom leaned over to give her a kiss – but their lips never met. A violent pounding on the windscreen made them jump out of their skins. A rain-soaked figure stood in front of the van, beating his fist on the glass and trying to see in. Suzie was furious. An important moment in her life had been ruined – and she knew just who was to blame.

It was Gordy.

Karlene always slept soundly. Like her friends, she worked hard at the hospital and was exhausted by the end of the day. Her eyes closed as soon as her head hit the pillow. She didn't hear the van arrive or depart. And she wasn't disturbed by the row between Gordy and Suzie. While her two friends were yelling at each other downstairs, Karlene was lost in her happy dreams.

She was walking across a desert. The hot sun was

beating down on her and her throat was like a furnace as she trudged on through the sand. She scanned the horizon but there was no sign of life or vegetation anywhere. She was out in the wilderness. She didn't even know if she was moving in the right direction or simply going round in circles. A huge sand dune confronted her and she began to climb it on all fours.

The next second, she was standing at the very top. Down below her was a large oasis, fringed with palm trees. The water looked cool and inviting. Karlene raced down the slope and flung herself onto the sand at the edge of the pool, bending over to drink the cool water. When her thirst was quenched, she scooped up more water in her cupped hands and threw it over her face. It was so refreshing.

She did it again and again — until she woke up with a start! This was no dream. Her face was indeed covered with cold water. So was her pillow and her bedclothes. Rain was pummelling the roof above her head and a steady drip was coming through the ceiling. It was like standing under a shower. Karlene was soaked.

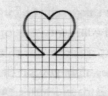

Chapter Four

Gordy gritted his teeth before he turned the corner. He'd got up early so that he could check out the damage to his car in daylight. As he walked into the cul-de-sac he shuddered. The Vauxhall Astra was a pitiful sight. It stood crushed up against the brick wall at the far end of the street. Glass splinters from the headlights seemed to be everywhere and one of the front tyres was punctured.

Even worse, Gordy had to walk past a series of parked cars, gleaming vehicles whose owners clearly took pride in them. Compared to them, the Astra looked like a wreck and it made him feel sick. When he got to his car, he examined it thoroughly, wincing at each new dent or breakage that caught his eye. The cost of repairs would be horrendous, and the car might even be a write-off.

A short, stocky man came out of a nearby house. 'That yours?' he demanded, aggressively.

'Er, yes,' confessed Gordy.

'Get rid of the thing, will you!'

'Don't worry, I will, I will.'

'This isn't a tip ya know. Get rid of the car and sweep up the mess after you or I'll report you to the police.' He turned round and headed back into his house. 'Drunk drivers!' he growled over his shoulder.

Gordy was glad to see him disappear. There was no point in explaining that he'd only been the passenger and that the driver was teetotal. He made swiftly for the nearest garage and arranged for them to collect his car as soon as possible. He said he would ring them later to find out the estimate for the repairs.

Gordy strode off towards the hospital with mixed feelings. He was still very angry with Jo. She'd put both their lives at risk and caused massive damage to his car. The repairs would probably cost more than the car was worth. His first instinct was to ask Jo to pay half the bill. Since she'd been responsible for the crash, he felt she should help to recover the damage.

But on reflection, Gordy decided against asking her for money. She was only driving the car as a favour to him after all. When he remembered all the other occasions she'd got him and the Astra safely back home, he saw how much he owed her. His anger softened as he thought about how Jo must be feeling. She must be unwell. It was really the only explanation for her terrifying loss of control. Gordy decided to be sympathetic.

The other students were streaming into the medical school when Gordy arrived at the hospital and he exchanged cheerful greetings with his friends. As soon as he was inside, he saw Jo. She was chatting to some of the other girls, laughing happily and showing no signs of injury from the previous night. When Gordy came up to her, she smiled warmly at him.

'Could I have a word?' he asked.

'Of course,' she said, easily.

'Let's go over there.' He led her to a quiet corner of the entrance hall and studied her face. 'How are you, Jo?'

'Fine, thanks.'

'No problems?'

'None at all, Gordy.'

'No cuts, bruises or headaches?'

'What is this?' she said, laughing. 'A consultation?'

'Did you sleep all right, Jo?'

'Like a log, thanks.'

'I didn't. I tossed and turned for hours. I'm surprised you got a wink of sleep after what happened.'

'What do you mean? The lecture at St Catherine's? I enjoyed that. And the meal at the pub afterwards.'

'I'm talking about the drive home, Jo.'

'You remember nothing about that, Gordy,' she teased. 'You were out for the count.'

'Until you started hitting the kerb.'

'What are you on about?'

'The incident in the cul-de-sac. Where you crashed my car, Jo.'

'I did not!' she said, surprised and angry. 'I drove you to your house, helped you in, then walked on to my flat. You were so drunk, you didn't know what was going on, that's all.'

'I certainly felt the impact when we thudded into that wall.'

'What wall? Is this some kind of silly joke, Gordy?'

'You really don't remember, do you?' he said, looking at her carefully. 'You've put the whole thing out of your mind.'

'What whole thing?'

'The accident, Jo.'

'There was no accident,' she insisted.

'Then how come the Astra is all smashed up?'

'Maybe a joyrider took it.'

'Yes,' he said, irritably. 'And her name was Jo Barnes.'

She stiffened. 'I don't find this very funny.'

'Neither do I, Jo. It's my car. The point is—'

'I've had enough,' she said, moving away. 'For the last time, I did not damage your car in any way. Now, will you please stop playing games!'

He stared after her. Gordy was more confused than ever.

The staff canteen was exceptionally busy at lunchtime and Mark and Bella had difficulty finding an empty table. Karlene soon joined them with her plate of salad. She was still annoyed about the way she'd been drenched during the night.

'It was like sleeping under a waterfall!' she groaned.

'The slates have been loose for ages,' said Mark. 'They've obviously finally slipped off the roof.'

'Poor old Karlene!' sighed Bella. 'Waking up in the dark to find yourself soaked to the skin.' She glanced at the window. 'At least it's stopped raining now.'

'Yes,' said Karlene, ruefully. 'But not before it did the damage. I had to spend the rest of the night sleeping on the floor, listening to the drips falling into the bucket I'd put under the leak. Ping! Ping! Ping!'

'Why didn't you wake one of us up?' asked Mark.

'No point in making you suffer as well. Thanks for going to investigate the leak, by the way, Mark. At least we know what the problem is now you've climbed up into the roof space.'

'That reminds me. I must empty the pans I put up there. They'll be almost full up by now.' He forked a piece of sausage into his mouth. 'Still, they stopped the water coming down into your room again.'

'I know, Mark,' said Karlene, 'but there's a terrible stain on the ceiling and some of the plaster has come down. It'll need to be repaired.'

'That's beyond me, I'm afraid.'

'It's the landlord's responsibility,' observed Bella. 'Get on to Mr Foss and complain.'

Karlene made a face. 'We know what he'll say.'

'He'll try to wriggle out of it.'

'Yes,' agreed Mark. 'We've been complaining about that roof for weeks and he's done nothing at all. Maybe we should just get it repaired and send him the bill.'

'He'd never pay it,' said Bella.

'We'll force him,' vowed Karlene. 'I ought to get compensation for last night. It was awful.'

They munched their food in silence for a few minutes. Then Mark put down his knife and fork. He pushed his spectacles up the bridge of his nose and grinned.

'I've got a better idea,' he said.

'Me too,' moaned Karlene. 'We move out.'

'No. We set Suzie on to him.'

'Yes,' said Bella, approvingly. 'It was Suzie who found the house in the first place. She's done all the negotiating with the landlord. Set her on to old Fossy.'

'She knows how to handle him,' said Mark.

Karlene smiled grimly. 'Both hands around his

throat?' she suggested.

'That's the answer,' continued Bella. 'Let the expert negotiator take over. Suzie will soon get him to do what we want.'

The decision was made. Now they could enjoy their lunch break. Or so they thought.

No sooner had they started to eat than they were interrupted by an ear-splitting noise. It was the fire alarm. Panic seemed to erupt all around them. Most people seemed to have forgotten everything they'd been taught during the few fire drills they'd experienced. They left their tables, running and pushing each other to get to the nearest exit, fighting to get out as quickly as possible.

Mark, Bella and Karlene were caught up in the crowd. It was frightening. But their concern soon became less for themselves and more for the patients. Everybody in the canteen was fit enough to get out on their own two legs. But some of the patients would be trapped in their beds, feeling really terrified. They were the ones in real danger from a fire.

When they eventually got out into the corridor, the three friends decided to see if they could help evacuate the patients. First of all, they had to establish where the fire had broken out in the main block. Swept along by the crowd, they got to the stairs then peeled off from the body of people going down.

'It's not on this floor!' shouted Mark.

'And there's no smoke coming up the stairs,' cried Karlene. 'I don't think it's down there.'

'Then it must be upstairs,' decided Bella.

The clanging bell stopped as instantly as it started. An ear-tingling silence followed, then an authoritative voice came over the tannoy explaining that it had been a false alarm.

The three friends were relieved, but they found they were shaking, still shocked. There might be no fire but the feeling of alarm had been far from false.

Gordy met Suzie at the end of the afternoon as she came out of the main hospital block. She wasn't pleased to see him and pushed past him roughly. Undeterred, Gordy fell into step beside her.

'Suze!' he coaxed.

'Go away, Gordy!'

'We need to talk.'

'I haven't got time now.'

'But I want to apologise.'

'It's a bit late for that, Gordy.'

Suzie started striding ahead of him but Gordy reacted swiftly. Running ahead of her, he turned to block her path with his arms outstretched. There was no way past him. Running her hands through her hair in frustration, she stopped in front of him.

'You're not leaving the hospital until this is settled,' he said.

'There's nothing to settle,' she said with dignity. 'I just never want to speak to you again, that's all.'

'Suze.'

'And don't turn on that false charm. It makes me want to throw up!'

'I thought we were friends.'

'So did I.'

'Please!' he begged.

Suzie took a deep breath and tried to stay calm.

'Look,' she explained. 'I said all there was to say last night. What you did was unacceptable.'

'I thought you might be in trouble inside that van.'

'You had no right to bang on the windscreen like that.'

'But what if he'd been harassing you?'

'It would have been none of your business.'

'I was just trying to help, Suzie.'

'Tom must've thought I was sharing a house with a lunatic. No wonder he drove off so quickly.'

'He wasn't really your type, anyway, was he?'

'How do you know?' she exploded, her cheeks turning scarlet with anger. 'I choose my own friends. I don't need you to check them out for me. Have I ever crashed in on you like that?'

'No, you haven't.'

'Then just think what it would be like. It was

humiliating. How would you like to be having an intimate conversation with a girlfriend in your car and some loony friend starts banging on the windscreen and shouting at you? It was so embarrassing!'

He swallowed hard. 'This has really got to you, hasn't it?'

'You could say that!'

'Can't we be friends again?'

'Not a chance!'

'I've never seen you as angry as this, Suze.'

'If you don't get out of my way, you'll see me a lot angrier. I will not be spied on, Gordy!'

'It won't happen again. Honestly.'

'I'm going home. Move out of my way, will you?'

'Don't charge off like this, Suzie.'

'I won't ask you again,' she warned.

'At least give me a smile,' he pleaded. 'That's all I ask. One small smile.'

Suzie glared at him with such intensity that he stepped quickly out of her way. Then her expression changed completely. She began to smile. It started at her lips and spread to her eyes, then covered the whole of her face. Gordy grinned in relief. He'd got through to her at last. Or so he thought. That was until he realised that Suzie was looking straight past him at someone else.

Tom Peterson was waiting for her at the gate.

'Hi, Suzie,' he said as he strolled over.

'Tom! It's great to see you!'

'I was hoping to catch you.'

'I've just finished.'

'In that case, are you free for a drink?'

'Well, yes… I suppose I am.'

'Then what are we waiting for?' Suzie walked off beside him. 'By the way,' Tom said, raising his voice, 'who was that prat who was thumping my windscreen last night?'

Gordy felt terrible. Jo had parted with him crossly, Suzie had refused to talk to him and he still had to get the news about his car from the garage. It just wasn't his day.

Bella was glad when the tutorial was over. Sister Killeen had been at her most sarcastic and she had borne the brunt of it. Mark tried to console her as they packed up their things. His moral support was always there when she needed it. She kissed him gratefully on the cheek.

'Let's forget Sister Killeen.' She sighed. 'Her bark's a lot worse than her bite. Now, tell me about this marathon.'

'There's not long to go now.'

'Are you fit enough? Twenty-six miles is a long way to run.'

'I'll manage it somehow, Bella. I have to.'

'Why's it so important to you, Mark?'

'I want to get the maximum amount of money from my sponsors. I've got a couple of dozen now.'

'Mark, that's fantastic.'

'Not really. Some of them have only sponsored me ten pence a mile.'

'Skinflints! If you complete the course and everyone coughs up, how much will you raise?'

'Over a hundred quid.'

'That would be fantastic!'

'And over a quarter of that will be from Gordy.'

'Don't bank on that,' she warned. 'If he has to pay for all the repairs to his car, he'll be broke. Hey, I don't suppose you've thought of asking Sister Killeen?'

'She was the first person I asked. She's on the list for twenty pence a mile.'

'Wonders will never cease!'

They were crossing the car park now and had reached the gate in time to see Suzie climbing into the battered Stress van. Tom was holding the door open for her. Once they were both inside, the van pulled away into the traffic.

Bella looked after them, amazed. She pointed at the disappearing van.

'Was that him?'

'Yes. Tom, the vocalist and lead guitarist of Stress.'

'He's a real hunk. Why haven't I been introduced?'

'I think Suzie wants to keep him to herself, Bella.'

'I'm not surprised,' she said. 'If I was lucky enough to be in a van with him, I wouldn't come out for a week! I'm going to find a way to meet that guy. Just you watch me!'

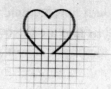

Chapter Five

Gordy went back to the medical school to use the public telephone. He steeled himself to hear the worst as he rang the garage and asked to speak to the Service Manager. Soon a gruff male voice came on the line.

'How can I help you, sir?'

'My car was towed in this morning. A Vauxhall Astra.'

'One moment…'

Gordy heard the receiver being put down as the man shuffled through some invoices. Then he heard a muted chuckle. The Astra had obviously given them a good laugh down at the garage.

'Here we are, sir,' said the manager, coming back on the line. 'Don't see many as old as that on the road. Surprised it passed its MOT.'

'What's the damage?'

'Quite extensive, I'm afraid. You're going to need a

new bumper, new radiator, new headlights, new—'

'Forget the list,' interrupted Gordy, depressed enough already. 'Just give me the cost, please.'

'Well, you're looking at almost nine hundred quid.'

'What!'

'That includes labour and materials.'

'I could buy another car for that.'

'Exactly, sir.'

There was a long pause as Gordy took in the full story. He could never afford that amount out of his grant and Jo wasn't insured. He could feel himself getting angry with her all over again.

'Do you want us to go ahead, sir?' asked the manager. 'There's the towing charge as well, of course.'

'I need time to think it over,' said Gordy in a panic. 'I'll be in touch. Goodbye.'

He slammed down the receiver and leant against the wall for support. It was true that his car had seen better days but he'd be lost without it. Apart from anything else, it added to his status among the other medical students. Girls tended to be more interested in you if you had a car. At least, that's what Gordy told himself.

He was about to go home when he remembered that he'd left his briefcase in the library. He trudged slowly up the stairs feeling completely despondent. And he wasn't cheered by seeing who was in the library. Jo was sitting at the far end, poring over a medical textbook, making notes. Gordy made a huge effort to control his anger before walking quietly down the room towards her.

She looked up as he came towards her. Although she looked quite pale and tense, Gordy thought, she smiled in her usual friendly way. 'Hi, Gordy. Are you coming to revise in here as well?'

'Not this evening, no.'

'We've got exams next week, remember?'

'There's something more important on my mind at the moment. It's my car.'

Her smile vanished. 'Don't start all that again, Gordy!'

'I have to, Jo.'

'It was nothing to do with me, you know that.'

'Listen, Jo, it was, I swear.'

'You must be crazy to think I'd forget a thing like that.'

Their raised voices brought a reproachful glare from the librarian. Other students were studying and the Silence rule had to be observed. Gordy resorted to sign language and began beckoning Jo to come outside. Eventually, she agreed to go.

Once out in the corridor, Gordy changed tack.

'Look, I'm sorry to bother you again, Jo,' he made his voice sound calm. 'I promise I won't keep you out here long. You obviously don't remember last night, do you?'

'Yes, I remember it very well, Gordy.'

'Then can we go through it, stage by stage?' he asked her.

'Do we have to?' she sighed.

'Just to please me, Jo, OK?'

'Right,' she said. 'First, we heard Gilbert Buchanan give the lecture, then we went to the pub for a meal. You had two glasses of wine and four pints of beer.'

'Then we set off in my car and—'

'And you fell asleep.'

'So far so good. It's the next bit that's the problem.'

'Only for you,' she pointed out. 'I've got a very clear recollection. I drove you home, just like I've done before, many times, helped you into the house then walked to my flat.'

'Is that what you really believe happened?'

'It is what happened, Gordy.'

'Suppose I tell you you're completely wrong? That I have a lot of evidence to prove it?'

'What do you mean? Is this some kind of joke?'

'Well, there's my car, for a start. I had to have it towed to the garage and they told me just now there's almost nine hundred quids' worth of damage. If it was OK when you parked it, how come it's a wreck now?'

'Who knows? Maybe you went out again in it last night and had an accident. Why are you trying to blame it on me?'

Gordy was worried. Jo clearly thought she was telling the truth. All memory of the crash had been wiped out of her mind. He made a conscious effort to be more gentle with her.

'Would you believe me if I had some witnesses? Bel and Kar, for instance. They saw me when I got back last night. They know I didn't come home in the Astra and they'll tell you what a state I was in.'

'You always are when you've drunk too much,' she said with feeling.

'I was pretty sober after the crash, I can tell you. Do you remember the crash in that cul-de-sac? There are people who saw that happen.'

'What people?' Jo was beginning to look upset and confused.

'The people who live in that street,' he said, softly. 'When we hit that wall there was a tremendous bang and they all came running out to see what had happened. They'll say they saw you behind the wheel.'

'They couldn't have, Gordy. I wasn't there!'

'You were, Jo, honestly, you really were. Speak to Bella and Karlene.'

'They're friends of yours – they're bound to say what you tell them to. Are they both in on this joke as well?'

'It's not a joke or a trick or anything like that, I promise you.'

'You'll just have to prove it then. Suzie's the only

51

person in your house I really trust. I might believe you if she tells me the same story. Ask her to have a word with me.'

'We-ell, that's a bit tricky,' said Gordy, uneasily. 'You see, we've fallen out.'

'I see. You mean she won't go along with this crazy joke of yours, is that it?'

'It's not that at all, I swear it!'

Gordy tried to explain again and calm Jo down but by now she was angry as well as confused. She looked defiantly at him.

'Well, you may not need to revise, but I do. Now just get out of my way – just leave me alone, will you?' And she pushed past Gordy and into the library. He was really concerned now. There must be something seriously wrong with Jo to make her behave like this.

They were at the same table in the same bar. Suzie and Tom clinked their glasses together before drinking. Suzie thought she'd probably never see him again after what Gordy had done, so she was really pleased to be with him.

'Sorry about last night,' he said. 'Charging off like that. I suddenly realised how late it was and had to get back to the club to pick up the others. Trudi gets a bit stroppy if I keep them hanging around.'

'Who's Trudi?' asked Suzie.

'She's our drummer. You know, the blonde one?'

'Oh, yes.' Suzie pictured the attractive girl in her mind. 'What did she say when you got back?'

'She gave me an earful – but I'm used to that. Trudi tends to be possessive. She expects me to be there when she needs me. She didn't like it when I went off without telling her.'

Alarm bells went off in Suzie's mind. She sensed she had some competition in Trudi. And she would definitely have the advantage over Suzie – she belonged to Tom's world, and she did not.

'Sorry – I hope it didn't look too rude,' said Tom.

'No, not at all. I thought Gordy had scared you off. You know, the face at the windscreen?'

Tom laughed. 'He did make me jump at first. Then I saw he was just an over-protective friend of yours.'

'Not any more!' she said to herself.

'The important thing is, we're together again. And I must say, you look great in that uniform, Suzie.'

'Not quite the thing for a bar, though, is it?' she laughed.

Tom flashed one of his stunning smiles at her and Suzie's doubts began to evaporate. If Tom had made such an effort to see her, he must be really keen. She had only one query.

'Does Trudi know you're here?' she asked, in as off-hand a way as she could manage.

'No, no, I didn't bother to tell her. She likes to try

and run my life for me and I need to be more independent than that. I've always been a bit of a maverick.' He put his hand on her arm. 'Now. Tell me everything you've done since we were last together. I want to hear all the gruesome details.'

'You'd be bored to death, Tom.'

'No I wouldn't. Just try me.'

His curiosity about her seemed endless. He listened intently to the description of her day at the hospital and asked questions in all the right places. Suzie felt a growing sense of closeness with him.

'That's enough about me. What have you been up to?' she said at last. 'Tell me what you've been doing since last night.'

'That's easy. Sleeping.' He grinned.

'All day?'

'Most of it, yeah. Then we had a rehearsal. Then on here.'

'Have you got another gig tonight?'

'No. We're rehearsing our songs tonight so that we're ready for tomorrow. That's our big day. We're in the recording studio.'

Suzie was impressed. 'You're making a record?'

'A demo tape. There's a record company that's keen to sign us up but they want to be sure we've got enough material. So we've hired the studio for the whole day.'

'Will the record company give you a contract then?'

'Maybe. Then Stress will become rich and famous!'

'You deserve it, Tom,' said Suzie, basking in reflected glory.

'I'll believe it when it happens.' Tom finished his drink. 'Well, I'll have to make tracks. Can I give you a lift back to your house?'

'Don't worry, I can take a bus.'

'Why bother when the Tom Peterson Courtesy Van is at your service? Drink up, you'll be back home in a couple of minutes.' He grinned. 'As long as you can guarantee that Gordy won't break my windscreen when I kiss you goodbye.'

'If he does, I'll kill him!' said Suzie gleefully.

She swallowed the rest of her wine and followed him to the door. When they were out on the pavement, he turned to face her.

'I meant to ask you,' he said, casually. 'Would you like to sit in on some of the recording session?'

'Wow!' Suzie breathed.

'I know you're at the hospital all day but we'll still be at it around this time tomorrow. So why don't you come along then, Suzie?'

'That would be great, if I won't be in the way.'

'I insist,' he said, putting an arm around her shoulders. 'Come on. Hop in and I'll give you the details on the drive back.'

Suzie felt as though she was floating on cloud nine all over again.

Mark clambered up through the trap door, banging his head on one of the rafters. He switched on the torch and let its beam play across the whole of the roof space.

'What can you see?' called Karlene from the landing.

'A huge great hole.'

'Are those pans full of water now?'

'Almost. I'll pass them down to be emptied.' The torch picked out another gap in the slates. 'Looks like we have another problem up here as well.'

'What is it?' asked Bella, who'd joined Karlene down below.

'Climb up the ladder and I'll show you.'

'No thanks,' she shuddered. 'I hate spiders.'

'There are no spiders up here,' Mark assured her. 'A few mice and bats, maybe. That's all.' He laughed as he heard Bella's muffled shriek of alarm. 'I was only joking. Come on up.'

'I'll stay down here, thanks.'

Bella was with Karlene in her bedroom, staring up at the large ugly stain on the ceiling. The fallen plaster had been swept up that morning but more had come adrift during the day.

'This room isn't fit to sleep in, Karlene,' said Bella. 'You can share with me, if you like.'

'If it rains again, I might just do that, thanks.'

There was a loud bang and a yell from the loft.

'What happened?' called Karlene.

'I forgot to duck,' said Mark. 'I've got the first pan of water in my hand. Are you ready?'

'Hold on!' shouted Bella.

She and Karlene went out on to the landing. A small ladder gave access to the trap door in the ceiling. Bella climbed halfway up to take the pan and passed it down to Karlene. Then Karlene emptied it into the bath. And so it went on until two more pans of rainwater had been disposed of. Then Mark re-positioned them under the hole in the slates.

The girls stood back as he climbed down the ladder. His clothes were covered in dust and there were cobwebs in his hair. He brushed them away.

'It's in a terrible state up there,' he said. 'It looks as if some of the rafters are rotten. If we're not careful, we'll have the whole roof down on our heads.'

'That settles it then,' decided Karlene. 'Action!'

'Yes,' said Bella. 'Over to Suzie. I thought I heard the front door a few minutes ago. It's probably her. Let's go and set her on to the landlord.'

'Wait for me,' said Mark, dusting himself off. 'I can give her a more accurate idea of what needs to be repaired.'

They found Suzie in the kitchen. She was standing there dreamily, still feeling Tom's kiss on her mouth.

'We're really glad to see you,' said Mark.

'Yes,' added Bella. 'We've got an emergency. There are holes in the roof and rotting timbers. We need repairs right away. Will you get onto Mr Foss at once?'

'Why?' said Suzie with a shrug.

'Because he's our landlord. He should pay for the repairs.'

'Well you can tell him that when you see him, Bella.'

'Who? Me?'

'Or Mark. Or Karlene. Or Gordy. Why should I always be the one to fight it out with Mr Foss? It's not fair.' Suzie folded her arms defiantly. 'I've got other things to do. It's high time one of you took some responsibility.'

'But you know how to deal with Mr Foss,' urged Karlene.

'Yes. I open my mouth and the words come out. You try it.'

Chapter Six

By next morning, the shock still hadn't worn off. As Mark ran through the streets at a steady pace, he was truly puzzled by Suzie's attitude. She usually thrived on responsibility. She loved taking control and organising others. All five of them paid the same rent and did an equal share of the domestic chores but Suzie was their leader. Until now that is. What could have made her change, he wondered.

Mark was wearing a sweatshirt, shorts and running shoes. His stride was low and economical, covering the ground with no undue effort. The marathon was not a race to him; his sole aim was to complete the course so that he could claim the sponsorship money. Working at the hospital had taught him the value of a scanner. It could identify all sorts of medical conditions at an early stage and so save lives. Mark was taking on this challenge to help others.

Suzie had encouraged him from the start. She

knew that he was a good athlete and had been in the cross-country team at school. On his first few training runs, she had paced him on a bicycle. But now he was getting up much too early for her. Of all his friends, Suzie was the most supportive. She was consistent, that's why her refusal to negotiate with the landlord on their behalf was so uncharacteristic. Mark had never known her show such indifference.

He rounded the corner and began the final half-mile home. He saw the hospital on his left. All the lights were on, shining through the grey dawn, and an ambulance was arriving, just as another was speeding off to an emergency. Whatever time he ran past the building, it was bustling with activity. That's what appealed to Mark about his career in nursing. There was always something happening.

Lengthening his stride, he went on past the hospital and down a slight gradient. He was running comfortably, and well within himself, when he spotted a figure ahead of him and slowed as he approached her. Mark realised it was Jo. Clutching her bag under her arm, she was walking purposefully along the pavement. He soon overtook her.

'Hi!' he said, stopping beside her, panting.

'Ah!' She came to a dead halt. 'You gave me such a fright, coming up behind me like that.'

'Sorry, Jo.'

She peered at him. 'Do I know you?'

'It's Mark, remember? I share a house with Gordy.'

'Oh, yes,' she said, sounding vague. 'What are you doing out so early?'

'Training for the marathon. You've probably seen the posters. They're all over the hospital. It's a sponsored run, to raise money for a new scanner.'

'That's a great idea!' she said, as if it was the first time she'd ever heard of it. 'Well done, Mark!'

'Thanks.' He looked at her more closely. Jo seemed as pleasant as ever but there was a confused expression on her face. It was as if she was in a daze.

'Have you recovered from the other night?' he asked.

'What do you mean?'

'You know, the accident – in Gordy's car. You and he crashed into a wall when you were driving him home.'

'No we didn't,' she said hotly.

'Well, that's what he told us, Jo.'

'That's what he told me as well, but it's a joke, some sort of game he's playing on me. I don't remember any car accident.'

'But you must, surely?'

'No I don't, Mark. Honestly.'

'Then how did the Astra get smashed up like that?'

'Don't ask me.' She looked mystified. But her denial was far less confident this time. She had a trapped and bewildered expression in her eyes and

Mark was worried about her.

'Why are you up at this hour?' he asked her, trying to change the subject.

'I want to put in a couple of hours of revision before my day begins.'

'Where? At the medical school?'

'Yes,' she explained. 'The library never closes. This is the best time to get in, when nobody else is around. I was on my way to the hospital when you caught up with me.'

'But you can't have been, Jo. You're walking in the wrong direction. The hospital's back there.'

'No, it isn't. It's this way.'

'Look, I've just come past it,' he said, pointing. 'Up on the right. The main hospital block.'

When Jo saw the hospital, she seemed frightened and disoriented. She looked up and down the road, pulling at her hair and trying to work out where she was. Mark could see her confusion.

'Jo,' he said gently, 'you walk to the medical school every day, why can't you find your way there this morning?'

Her face went blank. Her eyes darted nervously.

'I just don't know, Mark. I just don't know.'

Bella fancied a boiled egg but Karlene chose a grapefruit for breakfast. Both were still in their dressing gowns as they sat at the kitchen table.

'I'm glad the rain held off last night,' said Bella.

'So am I,' agreed Karlene. 'I don't want to lie listening to that endless drip-drip-dripping ever again.'

'Does your room still smell damp?'

'Yes, Bella. I had to open the window to let in some fresh air. And I've moved my bed from under the leak.'

'You shouldn't have to put up with it, Karlene.'

'I don't intend to for much longer.'

'We must tell the landlord. We'll just have to persuade Suzie to go round there and see him. It's her job, anyway.'

'It has been in the past,' said Karlene, reasonably. 'But only because the rest of us were too lazy or too cowardly to take our turn. Suzie was right. Why should she always have to do the dirty work?'

'Because she's so good at it.'

'Try telling her that.'

'I did,' said Bella, rolling her eyes. 'And she gave me a mouthful. It's unlike Suzie. What's got into her, do you think?'

'I'll give you one guess.'

'You don't mean?'

'What else?'

'But she's only known him five minutes.'

'You've been known to fall for a guy after five seconds!'

Bella giggled. 'That's different. I'm experienced. I've learnt to make up my mind instantly. Suzie's not like that.' She lowered her voice. 'Let's face it, Karlene. We've all had serious relationships since we've been at the hospital. You, me, Gordy — even Mark. But not Suzie.'

'Until she met Tom Peterson. She's really falling for him.'

'And it rebounds on us,' said Bella, sipping her coffee. 'We've lost our rock-solid, do-anything-for-you Suzie and we've got the couldn't-care-less version now.'

'Don't exaggerate, Bella!'

'Well! She's putting Tom before us.'

'You're a great one to talk!' said Karlene, laughing. 'When you're going out with a new boyfriend, you hardly notice the rest of us. Suzie's just… preoccupied, that's all. We should make allowances.'

'Not me, Karlene. I'm going to rescue us from the new Suzie. The one with her head in the clouds. If I lure this Tom away from her.'

'Don't you dare, Bella!'

'I'd be doing us all a favour.'

'No, you wouldn't,' said Karlene, firmly. 'Suzie would be shattered and then you'd be the one ignoring your friends. Just keep out of this. Let it take its own course.'

'But I really fancy him, Karlene.'

'Tough! Suzie met him first. So don't move in on him. She'd never forgive you.' Karlene finished her grapefruit and put it aside. 'As for the roof, I'm the one who ought to confront Mr Foss. It's my bed which got rained on and my face which got soaked.'

'That's true,' said Bella.

'I've got to fight my own battles,' Karlene went on, 'so I'll go and see that miserable landlord of ours this evening.'

'Then I'll come with you. Two are better than one.'

'Thanks, Bella. We'll pin him to the ground.'

The door opened and Mark came into the room, panting from his exertions and flopping down in the nearest empty chair.

'How was the run?' asked Karlene.

'Good fun,' he gasped. 'It's getting much easier.'

'Shall I make you some coffee?' volunteered Bella.

'No thanks. I'll have a glass of water when I get my breath back.' He sat up straight, inhaling deeply. 'Do you know who I just met? Jo Barnes. Over in the main street. She was making an early start so she could fit in some revision in the library.'

'She always was a bit of a swot,' noted Bella. 'Gordy says she'll be top of her year in the exams.'

'Only if she finds her way to the hospital to take them,' said Mark. 'She walked right past it today without even noticing it was there. I think there's something really strange about her.'

'The aftereffects of the accident, perhaps,' suggested Karlene.

'Yes,' added Bella. 'It was a truly nasty experience. Being stuck in a smelly old car with smelly old Gordy. No wonder Jo's in a daze. I'd have to go to bed for a week.'

'It's no joke, Bella,' said Mark, seriously. 'Jo was really weird. Sort of spaced out. She didn't seem to know where she was. I think she needs help.' He crossed to the sink to pour himself a glass of water. 'Right. I need a bath. I've been thinking about it all the way home.'

'Bad luck!' said Bella. 'Suzie's in there. She's seeing Tom this evening so she's giving herself the full treatment. Karlene and I've been waiting to get in that bathroom for ages. You'll just have to take your turn in the queue.'

Mark groaned as he slumped back into his chair.

'I'm surprised at you, Suzie,' said Geraldine Hobson. 'Aren't you feeling well today?'

'I'm fine, thanks,' said Suzie.

'It wasn't your first lapse of concentration, either. The X-ray equipment is extremely expensive. It must be treated with great respect.'

'I understand that, Mrs Hobson. I'm sorry.'

'By its very nature, radiography involves a degree

of radiation. Even though it's kept at a low level, we can't take any chances with it or patients could be put at risk.'

Suzie was contrite. 'I know. I really am sorry.'

'You pressed the wrong button at the wrong time.'

Geraldine Hobson was Suzie's tutor. She was a senior radiographer with years of experience, and was a patient and persuasive teacher who knew just how to bring out the best in her students. Suzie was the most promising trainee in her year and Geraldine had had to discipline her three times in the course of the day.

'You must keep your mind on the job, Suzie,' she emphasised.

'I will,' promised Suzie, glancing up at the clock on the wall. 'May I go now, please?'

'What's the hurry?'

'May I, Mrs Hobson? I've got an urgent appointment.'

Her tutor sighed and nodded. Suzie left her office quickly. She went straight to her locker in the changing room and took off her uniform. A few minutes later, she was swinging out through the hospital gates in a black sweater, jeans and boots. Suzie wanted to look attractive but casual. Large silver hoops hung through her ears and she'd let out her hair so that it fell long and red and shiny on to her shoulders.

She'd been thinking about the recording session all

day. She was very excited and she regretted having to let down her tutor. But this was one occasion when radiography took second place. Tom came first today. She couldn't wait to see him singing and performing. The recording studio was a couple of miles away and the bus seemed to take an age to get there. Frightened that she might be too late and miss all the action, she ran all the way from the bus stop.

Nirvana Studio was a disappointment. It sat in a converted warehouse at the end of a dingy street. The whole area was run-down and covered by a pall of smoke from a nearby factory. The studio itself had none of the glamour she'd imagined. It was adjacent to a scrap metal dealer and a large Alsatian barked at her from behind a wire-mesh fence.

Suzie was relieved when she was let into the safety and quiet of the studio. Tom had left word that she was to be allowed into the control booth, but she was given no more than a glance when she came in. The four people in the booth were bent over their equipment, making minute adjustments as the sound of the music pounded and throbbed around them. Stress were playing one of their best-known songs. Wearing earphones, all five were looking pale and tired but they were still putting tremendous energy into their number. Evidently, it had been a long and tiring day at the studio.

Suzie felt like an intruder. Everyone in the booth

ignored her and the only person in the group who paid her any attention was Trudi, the drummer. As their eyes met, Trudi glared at her with a hostile expression, then hit her drums with increased ferocity. Suzie wasn't welcome. After making such an effort to get to the studio, she was overwhelmed by a sense of disappointment. She was an outsider. She shouldn't be there and she began to wonder if she should sneak out again quietly, without anybody noticing.

Just then, Tom looked up and saw her for the first time. He looked straight into the booth and his face glowed with pleasure. He carried on singing but now he directed the words only at Suzie. It was as if he was dedicating the number to her. Tom wanted her there and that was all that mattered. Suzie could listen to him for ever.

Chapter Seven

Gordy watched her carefully all day. There was definitely something wrong with her. On the surface, Jo was her usual, cheerful self, smiling and pleasant to all her friends. But Gordy could see cracks appearing in her manner and he resolved to tackle her again. At the end of their day at the medical school, he intercepted her coming out of the library.

'Have you got a moment, Jo?' he asked.

'Not really,' she said, looking wary.

'But this is important, Jo.'

'So is revising for the exam. I'm off home to study.'

'You can't spend all your time with your head in a textbook, it's not good for you.'

'I have to, Gordy,' she said, looking pale and tense. 'It's the only way I can catch up. I'm way behind.'

'What are you on about? You're the star of first year. You'll get brilliant grades. I'm the one who ought to be in a panic.'

'Then why aren't you?'

'Good question.' Gordy's stomach lurched at the very thought of the exam. 'You come first, Jo,' he said, trying to bring the focus back on her. 'Listen, why don't we slope off somewhere for a quiet drink and a chat?'

'Now?' Jo was staggered. 'You must be mad. Alcohol is the last thing I need.'

'I was thinking more of an orange juice in the canteen,' said Gordy, lamely.

'Look, Gordy, all I want to do is go home and work, get it?'

She moved away but he detained her with a gentle hand on her arm. He tried to sound persuasive.

'Maybe you're working too hard, Jo?'

'Let go of me! Out of my way, please Gordy.'

'Is there anything bothering you, Jo?'

'Yes!' she said. 'You are!'

'What I mean is – are you feeling very stressed at the moment?'

'Yes,' she said exasperated. 'I have this overpowering urge to hit you. What on earth's got into you, Gordy?'

'I just want to help. It's not just me. Mark noticed something as well. When he met you first thing this morning, you seemed to have forgotten where the hospital was. Mark said you were in a complete daze.'

'He couldn't have, I wasn't there.' She began to look cornered and confused.

'Mark was out on a training run when he spoke to you.'

'But he didn't! I came straight to the medical school this morning. I didn't talk to anyone.'

'Don't you remember meeting him?' said Gordy, even more alarmed now.

'Of course not. How could I when I didn't meet him?'

'Mark wouldn't make a mistake like that.'

'Then he's lying!' said Jo, vehemently. 'I didn't see him or speak to him today. I don't want to talk to Mark and I certainly don't want to talk to you.'

'Look Jo, aren't you worried that you can't remember these things?'

'Gordy…' she said, warningly.

'Let me explain again, please. First, you forget crashing my car into a brick wall. Then you can't remember talking to Mark. This is really serious, Jo. We should do something about it.'

'Stop teasing me! I've had enough!' Her voice was taut and edgy.

'But I'm not. Honestly, Jo.'

'If you say any more I'll scream!'

Jo was shaking now and her eyes were glazed and angry. It seemed to Gordy as though she was on the verge of some kind of breakdown. He stepped back. Everything he was doing seemed to make the situation worse. She needed time to calm down. He opened the door and stood aside, smiling apologetically.

Without another word, Jo ran out of the hospital into the stillness of the afternoon.

Suzie was mesmerised. She hadn't realised just how much hard work went into a recording session. When she'd reached Nirvana Studio, the band were working on their last song but it took ages to perfect. Under the direction of the producer, a young guy with a ponytail who was in the booth, Stress sang it again and again, varying it slightly each time. The engineers adjusted the controls to get the right balance between voices and instruments. Suzie was impressed by the professionalism of everyone involved. Only when the producer was satisfied, did he play the song back to the group.

Stress were exhausted but clearly pleased with the results of their session. Tom gave each of the girls a hug then waved wearily goodbye as they left the studio. After a long chat with the producer, he finally found a moment for Suzie. They stepped out into the corridor to talk.

'What did you think?' he said.

'I really loved it. It was fantastic and thanks for asking me.'

'Thanks for coming, Suzie. When I saw you in the booth, it really seemed to help me get through the last number. I felt shattered by then. We've been here all day,' he said with a tired grin. 'We're dead on our feet. I'm not sure we'll make it tonight. We've got another gig to do.'

Suzie gasped. 'On top of a session like that?'

'Crazy, isn't it? We need a week off to recover. But it's a good date and you have to take whatever chances come along. Another band dropped out at the last moment so Stress are filling the gap. The drag is the club's fifty miles away.'

'That's bad luck, Tom,' she said. 'A long drive after such an exhausting session here doesn't sound much fun.'

'We're not on till eleven. That'll give us time to grab something to eat and take a break. Then it's on stage for a good hour.'

'Will your voice hold out after today?'

'We'll put a few more instrumental numbers in. And the girls do a great song on their own. We'll get through somehow,' said Tom, ruefully.

'I wish I could be there to give you moral support.'

'So do I, Suzie. But the van's not big enough for more than five of us and our gear. Trudi's drum kit takes up most of the room. See if you can catch us at the next gig.'

'I'll try and do that, Tom. If you'd like me to.'

'Of course I would,' he said, putting his hands on her shoulders. 'You're my inspiration. It's a pity you couldn't hear more of the recording session. We were really good in there.'

'That's fantastic!'

Suzie grinned admiringly at Tom and he gave her a huge hug. It was a wonderful moment but their mood was quickly shattered when Trudi put her blonde head round the door.

'Get a move on, Tom!' she said, loudly. 'We're hungry.'

'I'll be there in a minute,' he said, letting go of Suzie.

'Come on!'

Trudi vanished and Tom glanced at his watch. He was reluctant to leave, but he knew he had no choice. Stress was everything to him, including his livelihood. It had to come first. Suzie knew exactly what he was feeling.

'You go,' she said, softly. 'Don't worry about me. I'll find my own way back. It's been worth coming just to hear that one song.'

Tom had a sudden inspiration. He put his hand in his pocket. 'Would you like to hear the demo tape, Suzie?' he asked.

She was delighted. 'I'd really like to, Tom!'

'As long as you promise you'll take care of it. Don't let it out of your sight. I need it back tomorrow so I can take it round to the record company. But you can keep it overnight.'

'I'll sleep with it under my pillow,' said Suzie, smiling.

'Here,' he said, handing over the tape. 'I know it'll be safe with you. I'll ring you at the hospital tomorrow, OK?'

Suzie was too excited to do anything but nod. Not only would she be able to listen to all the tracks that Stress had recorded, but tomorrow she'd be seeing Tom again. Suzie felt light-headed she was so happy.

They were leaving the hospital when it happened again. Bella and Karlene were about to cross the car park when the fire alarm went off in the main block. Again the reaction was instant. Panic seemed to prevail everywhere. People came running out of Reception and nurses moved swiftly into wards to comfort their patients as they attempted to evacuate them, and everyone else inside the building looked for the nearest fire exit.

The feeling of hysteria increased with the approaching wail of the fire engine. That really seemed to confirm that the fire was no joke and the two girls heard a few screams of terror. They were soon part of a large and frightened crowd, craning their necks to see where the fire was and then moving back in a wave to let the fire engine surge into the car park. As the firemen rushed into the building to search for the source of the blaze, the scream of the alarm ceased abruptly. The emergency appeared to be over. Was this another false alarm?

'I was really frightened that time,' admitted Bella, looking shaken.

'Me too,' said Karlene, her heart pounding. 'Thank goodness it wasn't for real.'

'That alarm was bad enough. What could be setting it off?'

'Who knows? Come on Bella, let's get away from here.'

The long walk from the hospital gave them plenty of time to rehearse what they were going to say to Foss. Karlene didn't just want to report the leak in the roof and the hole in her ceiling. She also wanted to tell her landlord about the cracked downpipe outside the kitchen. Bella thought of something else to add to their list.

'That faulty wiring in my room,' she said. 'When I switched my hair dryer on, the socket went off with a bang.'

'There're two other sockets that don't work, as well.'

'And that light on the landing.'

Mr Foss's house was in a tree-lined avenue. It was large and modern with a garden in front and a new Mercedes in the drive. As they looked up at the gleaming paintwork on the house, the girls thought of their own drab, neglected building. Their landlord clearly didn't mind spending money on his own home.

Alec Foss answered the door himself. He was a middle-aged man in a smart suit and a garish tie. Short, stout and balding with a pencil moustache under his bulbous nose, he looked rather intimidating to Bella and Karlene. Both girls were still in their hospital uniforms and the landlord gave them a brusque welcome.

'I don't care what you're collecting for,' he snapped. 'You're wasting your time.'

'We're not collecting for anything,' explained Bella.

'No,' added Karlene. 'I'm Karlene Smith and this is Bella Denton. We're your tenants from Coveney Street.'

'What number?' grunted Foss. 'I own three houses in Coveney Street.'

'Number twenty-five,' said Bella.

'Oh, yeah. The students from the hospital. Five of you. Suzie Hembrow usually comes here, doesn't she?' A defensive look came into his eyes. 'Well? What's the problem?'

'There are several things…' started Karlene.

'Yes, beginning with the roof,' said Bella.

'Some slates came loose and slipped down into the guttering. There's quite a big hole up there, Mr Foss. The other night the rain poured in through my ceiling. It's brought some of the plaster down, too.'

'So? What am I supposed to do about it?' he challenged.

'Mend the roof,' suggested Bella, bravely. 'You're the landlord.'

'It's in the contract, Mr Foss,' added Karlene.

'No, it isn't. My commitment is to maintain the house in reasonable order. That's what I've done. Before I let a property, I always do a full inspection to make sure it's in good nick. Then I keep a close eye on it.'

'But you've hardly been near the place since we moved in,' said Bella, jutting out her chin determined not to let him off the hook.

'I don't need to. That house is as sound as a bell.'

'It's got a hole in the roof and it's your job to repair it, Mr Foss.'

'You'll have to think again. I'm not forking out good money on something that's not essential.'

'But it is! The water's pouring in.'

'Then stick a bucket under the hole.'

'That's what we've done,' said Karlene. 'But it's only a temporary solution. We've been up in the loft and some of the roof timbers are rotting. They need replacing. Then there's some electrical work that's pretty urgent, too. And a cracked downpipe. You'd better come and see for yourself.'

'You'll just have to pay for the repairs yourselves,' said their landlord.

'We can't afford to, Mr Foss.'

'Well don't come bothering me,' he said, sharply. 'That house was in good condition when you moved in. You all signed the contract. If you don't like the place, there's a simple solution.'

'Oh yes?' said Karlene.

'Move out.' So saying, Foss gave them a grim smile and shut the door in their faces. Karlene and Bella found themselves staring at it in dismay.

Suzie was in a dazed and happy state on her bus ride back to the hospital. The demo tape was in her bag and she hugged it to her tightly. Tom had been really trusting to lend it to her. She knew how precious it was to him and it showed just how much he liked her. Suzie was determined not to let the tape out of her sight for a second.

As her personal stereo was at the hospital, she went straight back there to retrieve it from her locker. She was about to leave, when she saw Geraldine Hobson coming out of her office. Suzie paused, guiltily.

'Hello, Suzie,' said her tutor. 'You're back early.'

'I needed something from my locker,' explained Suzie, tapping her bag. 'Look, I'm sorry about... you-know-what.'

'That's all right, Suzie. Everyone has off-days.'

'It won't happen again, I promise. I'll be completely

on the ball tomorrow.'

'Good.' Geraldine's eyes twinkled. 'I hope he was worth all the effort. That's why you were in such a rush to leave, wasn't it?'

'Yes,' admitted Suzie with a grin. 'And he was.'

'See you in the morning then.'

Her tutor smiled and Suzie was relieved that she'd had a chance to explain what had happened earlier. She hated letting Mrs Hobson down and it wouldn't reflect well on her, either.

With her handbag slung over her shoulder, Suzie took a short cut through the main block so she could go out through the Outpatients' Department. It was busier than usual for that time of the evening. When she came out into the street, the light was fading fast and she couldn't wait to get home so that she could listen to the Stress tape.

But she didn't get far. Suddenly, without warning, someone jumped out of the dark and grabbed at her bag. Instinct made her hang on to the strap. She got a brief glimpse of an angry face as the guy breathed at her.

'Let go or I'll smash your face in!'

But Suzie clung on desperately. The demo tape was in the bag and Tom would never forgive her if she lost that. Even when the guy punched her, Suzie didn't release her grasp. He hit her again, harder, then tugged with such vicious force that she felt a searing pain in her fingers. She had to let go of the strap. The mugger darted off round the corner with her bag.

Suzie collapsed onto the pavement, shaking and in tears.

Chapter Eight

Mark was both mystified and disturbed. It was difficult to believe what Gordy had just told him.

'But I talked to Jo this morning,' he insisted.

'I'm sure you did, Marco.'

'Then why does she pretend we never even met? I think Jo's got real problems.'

'I tried to tell her that,' said Gordy, wincing at the memory. 'But she just wouldn't listen. She's convinced that she wasn't involved in any car crash and didn't chat to you early this morning.'

'Maybe she confused me with someone else.'

'No chance. Besides, she claims she didn't speak to a living soul on her way to the medical school.'

'Poor Jo!' sighed Mark.

'Poor old Gordy as well! She really gave me an earful!'

'Has she shown any other worrying signs?'

'Yes, she's tense, irritable and wandering around in

small circles. That's not the Jo Barnes that I know.'

'She needs professional help, Gordy.'

'That's what I tried to tell her.'

'This isn't something you could handle, Gordy,' said Mark. 'She ought to be consulting her doctor about these lapses of memory.'

'She won't admit that she's had them. That's the trouble. Jo doesn't remember not remembering, if you see what I mean. She won't recognise she has a problem.'

'Can't you persuade her to visit her GP?'

'No!' wailed Gordy. 'I couldn't persuade her to do anything. She's gone off me in a big way.'

'Perhaps I should have a chat with her?'

'She'd only deny everything, Marco. So we'd be right back where we started.'

They were in the living room at the house. Mark was sitting on the sofa and Gordy was pacing around, restlessly. Neither of them could understand Jo's behaviour. They thought in silence for a few minutes, then Mark slapped his thigh.

'The car accident!' he decided. 'Jo crashed your car into a brick wall.'

'I know that,' said Gordy. 'But she doesn't.'

'But that's when it must have happened, Gordy. Her loss of memory.'

'Then why don't I have it as well? I was sitting beside her in that car but I didn't forget all about it. I wish I could! It was terrible.'

'People react in different ways,' said Mark. 'Perhaps she was so terrified by the accident that she refuses to believe it ever happened.'

'But why was she so terrified meeting you this morning that she's pushed that out of her mind as well? No, that's not the answer. She started to freak out before the crash. She seems to be cracking up before my eyes. She's the last person you'd think wouldn't be able to cope with stress. It's awful to watch it. She's such a great girl, a real friend. I must help her somehow.'

Gordy flopped into a chair, his head in his hands. Their thoughts were interrupted by the sound of the telephone. Mark answered.

'Hi, Mark,' said an Australian voice. 'It's Damian here.'

'Oh hi, Damian. How are you?'

'Fine, thanks. Look, Suzie's in a bad way. That's why I'm ringing you.'

'Is she ill or something?' asked Mark with concern.

'No, she's been mugged.'

'Oh no! What happened? When was this?'

'About half an hour ago. Just outside the hospital. That was the one piece of luck; Suzie was right on the doorstep so we were able to bring her straight into Casualty.'

'Has she been hurt?'

Suzie? Injured? Gordy, listening, was getting alarmed.

'Two broken fingers,' explained Damian. 'I've put them in splints and taped them up. But Suzie's so shaken, I don't want to send her back on her own. That's why I'm calling you.'

'Thanks, Damian,' said Mark. 'I'm on my way.'

He banged down the receiver and grabbed his coat.

'What's going on, Mark?' demanded Gordy.

'We need to go and get Suzie. Now!'

The two of them were soon running towards the hospital.

Suzie was lying on the examination bed behind some screens. The punches from her attacker had left bruises on her face and arms, and her whole body was aching. Her fingers throbbed painfully. But the mental pain was worse. Her mind was racing as she imagined her meeting next day with Tom. What would he say when he realised that she'd let his precious demo tape get stolen? This would be the end of a beautiful relationship. It was all too horrible.

Dr Damian Holt stepped in through the curtains.

'How do you feel now, Suzie?' he asked.

'Pretty bad.'

'I've just spoken to Mark and he's coming over to collect you.'

'Thanks, Damian.'

'You need rest and quiet now, Suzie.'

'Not much chance of that!'

'Did you get a look at the mugger?'

'Yes,' she said with a shiver. 'He was so close to me, I'll never forget his face.'

'So you would recognise him again?'

'I think so, yes. He was about sixteen or seventeen.'

'It would have been better if you'd just let go of your bag. That's what the police always advise,' said Damian, gently.

'I couldn't!' she said, sitting up. 'It had something really valuable inside. And I know I've let him get away with it.'

'You were too brave for your own good, Suzie.'

'I had to try and hang on to it! I just had to!'

Damian tried to calm her down as tears welled up in her eyes again. She looked terrible and his heart went out to her. He led her to a small recovery room at the back of the Casualty Department where she sat on the edge of the bed with her mind still in turmoil. Damian put a sling around her neck to support her injured hand. Suzie was relieved that he was on duty – Damian was a friend and a very good young doctor. Suzie had got to know him during his on-off romance with Bella. It was so reassuring to see his kind face at this time. Damian adjusted the sling.

'Unfortunately, you're not the first victim we've

had recently. There's been a lot of petty theft around here in the last few weeks and Outpatients and Casualty are the main targets. Only last week one of the clerical staff was mugged right next to the hospital.'

'What about Security?'

'They've been alerted but they're understaffed. Hundreds of people come and go each day; Security can't keep tabs on them all.'

'I suppose not, no.'

There was a tap on the door and Mark and Gordy came in, gasping for breath after their dash to the hospital. When they saw Suzie's injuries, they were quite distressed.

'You poor thing!' said Gordy, putting his arm around her.

'What exactly happened?' asked Mark. 'Was there much in your handbag?'

'Give her some space, guys,' suggested Damian. 'Suzie's been through a nasty experience. She's still very shaken.'

'That mugger will be shaken when I get my hands on him!' vowed Gordy. 'Only the worst kind of coward attacks women.'

'How do you feel now, Suzie?' asked Mark.

'Angry with myself,' said Suzie, hanging her head sadly.

'It wasn't your fault.'

'It was, Mark. I should have been prepared.'

'But you don't expect to get mugged in the hospital grounds,' argued Gordy. 'You couldn't possibly have been prepared for this.'

'Just tell us what happened, Suzie, if you feel up to it,' added Mark.

'I will. On the way to the police station. I want to report it. That mugger was very violent. The sooner the police start looking for him, the better.'

'Look after that injured hand,' warned Damian.

'I will, and thanks again, Damian.'

With Mark and Gordy supporting her, Suzie left the hospital, painfully slowly.

By the time they got back to the house, the rain had started in earnest. Karlene and Bella went straight to the kitchen to pour themselves a restoring glass of cider. After their confrontation with the landlord, they felt they needed it.

'That man's a pig!' said Bella.

'Yes,' agreed Karlene. 'I really admire Suzie. She knows how to deal with Mr Foss — we don't.'

'The only way to deal with a man like that is with a sledgehammer. He made me so mad!'

'I could see that, Bella.'

'He was lucky I didn't vandalise his posh Mercedes.'

'That wouldn't have helped at all.'

'Maybe not. But it would have given me a lot of satisfaction. Just think, Karlene. Our rent helped to pay for that new car! We should have let his tyres down at least! We've got to get our own back somehow.'

'We will,' promised Karlene, opening the drawer of the cabinet and taking out a large envelope. 'With the help of this.'

'What's that?'

'Our contract with the landlord.'

'He didn't bat an eyelid when we mentioned that.'

'He was only bluffing. We must have some tenants' rights.'

Karlene took out the contract and began poring over it as she spread it out on the table. Bella had a long swig of her cider. But it did nothing to soothe her hostility towards her landlord.

'What a crook,' she said. 'What a dirty, rotten crook.'

'A clever crook,' corrected Karlene. 'That's why we've got to beat him at his own game. With the contract.'

'Suzie's the person to do that. Just when we need her, she's not here to help us. And why? She's too busy swooning over that pop singer.'

'Come off it, Bella. You fancied him as well.'

'True. I'd give him ten smoochy points!'

'Well, so does Suzie.' Her finger stopped on a line

in the contract. 'Good, here we are. I think we've got Mr Foss over a barrel. Listen. The landlord is responsible for the maintenance of the property and must pay for any repairs that become necessary. It can't be clearer than that, can it?'

'He'll try to wriggle out of it somehow, Karlene.'

'Not if I wave this contract under his nose. He won't get rid of us so easily next time, Bella. We'll win in the end.'

'To victory!'

They clinked glasses and drank some more cider, confident of success in the next round against their landlord. But the celebration was interrupted by a distant clang of metal.

'What was that?' said Bella.

'It sounded as if it came from upstairs.'

'Something falling over maybe.'

'Oh no!' cried Karlene. 'Not one of those pots in the loft! I knew I should have emptied them first thing.'

'We've had showers all day.'

'Please let it be someone else's ceiling this time!'

She leapt to her feet and ran upstairs with Bella hard on her heels. When she flung open her door and switched on the light, Karlene was horrified. The contents of a large pan of water had poured through a new hole in her ceiling. Her books, clothes and carpet were completely sodden. It was even worse than before. Karlene was dumbstruck but Bella found her voice at once.

'That stinking landlord is to blame for this!' she shrieked. 'Just wait till I get hold of him!'

It was a long wait for them at the police station. When Suzie had reported the crime and given a full statement, she was taken off by a WPC to look through some photographs in the hope that she might recognise her attacker. Gordy and Mark had to sit in the waiting room.

'I hate these places,' said Gordy, grimly.

'That means you've got criminal tendencies,' Mark joked. 'That's why you let an uninsured driver get behind the wheel of your Astra.'

'Keep your voice down, Marco!' hissed Gordy. 'You'll get me arrested. I'm in enough trouble over that car already.'

'Have you told your father about the crash yet?'

'I can't face it. He'd disown me.'

'Bad week, one way and another,' observed Mark.

'You can say that again!'

'Car crash, hole in the roof, Suzie mugged... not to mention Jo acting so strangely. I reckon we deserve some good news for a change.'

'What I need is a miracle, Marco!'

'How about a big win on the National Lottery?'

'Yes,' said Gordy, taking up the idea with relish. 'Then I could buy a new car, pay for the repairs to the house and reimburse Suzie for whatever was stolen.'

'What about Jo?'

'That's another story. I don't think we'll be able to solve her problems with money. I've got a feeling it'll take time, patience and masses of tender loving care.'

Mark nodded and looked up as Suzie approached. 'Finished?' he said.

'Yes, we can go now.'

'I was just planning how to dispose of my winnings on the lottery,' boasted Gordy. 'Forget about that old handbag. I'll replace everything that was in it.'

'If only you could, Gordy!'

'I'll buy you a brand new Walkman.'

'That's not what I need, Gordy. I don't mind so much about that, or about the money that was stolen. It's the tape. Tom trusted me with it. He'll be so mad with me when he finds out what's happened.'

'No he won't,' assured Mark. 'Tom will understand. You broke two fingers trying to save his tape. He'll be really sympathetic.'

'I'm not so sure,' said Suzie, looking pale and sad.

'Neither am I,' said Gordy, airily. 'These pop stars only think of themselves. My guess is he'll throw a tantrum and stalk out. You'll never see him again, Suzie. Just as well, really. He doesn't deserve you. Take my word for it – you're far better off without Tom Peterson.'

Mark poked him sharply in the ribs. As Gordy looked up he saw tears of despair in Suzie's eyes. She went quickly out of the room. Gordy's face was a picture of innocence.

'What did I say?' he wondered.

Chapter Nine

Bella made breakfast for both of them next morning. After a night sleeping on her friend's floor, Karlene felt stiff and tired. The second deluge had soaked her mattress so she couldn't use that in Bella's room. The floor had been hard and unyielding. Karlene smiled gratefully as Bella ladled out the hot porridge into two bowls.

'How are you feeling now?' asked Bella.

'Ready to kill that landlord.'

'If it wasn't for him, you'd have spent a comfortable night in your own bed.'

'With a ceiling above my head.'

'You could sue him for the damage to your books, Karlene.'

'I wish I could.' She reached for the sugar bowl and felt a twinge in her arm. 'Aouw! I'm aching all over.'

'What you really need is a hot bath and a massage.'

'You're right,' said Karlene. 'The trouble is, I'm the

only physio around here and I can hardly give myself a proper massage.'

'Why not ask one of the guys on your course?'

Karlene giggled. 'No, thanks. They'd get carried away.'

'That's all part of the fun,' said Bella, laughing.

They heard the front door open and shut and seconds later, Mark came into the kitchen in his running gear. There was perspiration on his face as he sat down heavily at the table.

'How far did you go this morning?' asked Bella.

'Break any world records?' teased Karlene.

'Can't hear you,' said Mark, removing the earphones from his ears. 'I've started to run to music. Takes all the sting out of it. The rhythm seems to carry me along.'

'Don't mention that to Suzie,' said Karlene. 'Pop music's a sore point at the moment. She's so annoyed with herself for losing that tape.'

'She didn't lose it,' Mark pointed out. 'It was stolen.'

'It comes to the same thing in Suzie's mind. The tape was in her safekeeping and now it's gone. She's dreading the moment when she has to face Tom at the hospital.'

'She's not going there today, surely?'

'Yes she is, Mark. She insists.'

'Suzie needs a few days off to rest that hand. That's what Damian advised.'

'Yes,' said Bella, seeing her chance to meet Tom. 'Suzie must have a day in bed. I'll see Tom on her behalf and explain what happened. That way, she'll be spared all the hassle.'

'And you'll be able to chat him up,' said Karlene with a chuckle. 'We know your tricks, Bella. Stop pretending you're doing Suzie a favour. You just want a chance to get at that guy yourself. Well forget it. Nothing will stop Suzie from meeting Tom. If she'd broken both legs, she'd still get to the hospital today.'

'Then why can't she come with us to Old Fossie?' said Bella, truculently. 'If she's well enough to go out, she can give us moral support when we tackle the landlord again.'

'Leave her out of this. Suzie's got enough on her plate.'

'Yes,' said Mark. 'If you want support, I'll come with you. But there's a much quicker way to contact Mr Foss. Why not just pick up the phone?'

'We tried that last night,' replied Bella. 'Every time we rang, we got an answering machine. Karlene wouldn't let me leave a message or it would've burned his ears off.'

'We need to see him face to face,' said Karlene. 'My room is a mess. He has to do something now.'

'I'm there if you need me,' volunteered Mark.

'Thanks. But we've had a close look at our rental agreement. Mr Foss doesn't have a leg to stand on.

We can force him to pay for those repairs.'

Karlene was supremely confident. The law was on their side.

♡

Suzie was in great discomfort throughout the morning. She had a bad headache and her injured hand throbbed painfully. The bruises on her face were another problem. Even though they were partly hidden by make-up, they were hideous. They certainly got her a lot of sympathy from her friends but they also attracted a lot of curious stares. It was embarrassing.

Losing the use of one hand was a serious handicap. It was an effort just to get dressed. She was such an independent girl that she hated having to ask for help, so she soldiered on as best she could. But at least it was the fingers on her left hand that had been broken and Suzie was right-handed.

She waited all morning for a phone call from Tom and she practised what she would say to him over and over again in her mind. There was no point in trying to deceive him. The tape had gone. She would just have to suffer the consequences. Tom was completely committed to his work with Stress and the theft of the tape would be a disaster. Suzie shuddered when she imagined what he would say to her.

But the phone call didn't come. She decided that he must be sleeping in after his late night at the gig. He would probably contact her that afternoon. While her colleagues went off to the canteen for lunch, Suzie stayed behind in the X-ray Department. She didn't want everyone peering at her bruised face, anyway. Instead, she hid away in the rest room for the student radiographers. She ate the apple and the piece of cheese she had brought with her.

Suzie was examining her face in the mirror when there was a tap on the door. It opened tentatively. She was amazed to see it was Tom.

'Tom!'

'Mrs Hobson said I'd find you here.' He saw her bruises and her injured hand. 'Suzie! What happened to you?'

'I was mugged,' she said, beginning to feel sick now he was here.

'Someone hit you?'

'Yes.'

'That's awful,' said Tom, putting his arm tenderly around her shoulders. 'Do they know who did it?'

'Not yet, no.'

'When they do, I'd like a word with him! Look at your face.' He led her to a chair. 'Come and sit down.'

'I'm fine, Tom. Really.'

'You should be at home in bed,' he said, easing her into the chair and crouching down beside her. 'Why did you come into the hospital today? Surely you should be on sick leave?'

'I wanted to be here when you rang.'

'I decided to come round instead,' he explained. 'When I asked for you in the X-ray Department, a Mrs Hobson told me to look in here. She didn't mention you'd been mugged.'

'I feel much better now.'

'Is there anything I can get you?'

'No, thanks. It's great just being here alone with you.'

He kissed her cheek and she began to feel reassured. Tom was kind and supportive. She'd been wrong to fear the worst. She should have had more faith in him.

'So?' he prompted. 'Tell me what happened.'

'When I left the studio yesterday, I came back here to fetch something. I was on my way out, when he jumped on me.'

'Was the mugger on his own?'

'Yes, Tom,' she explained. 'And he attacked me when I least expected it. Right outside the hospital.'

'Didn't anyone see him and come to your rescue?'

'It was over so quickly. He grabbed my bag but I wouldn't let go so he punched me, twice. Then he yanked the bag so hard that he broke two of my fingers.'

'I'll break every bone in his body!' Tom's eyes flashed dangerously.

'He disappeared in a minute. There was no hope of catching him. I ended up in a heap on the pavement.'

'Poor Suzie!'

His voice was so full of sympathy and affection that she was encouraged to break the bad news to him. Taking a deep breath, she blurted it out.

'Your demo tape was in my handbag, Tom.'

'What?'

'It was stolen along with everything else.'

He stood up. 'You let him get our tape?'

'I couldn't stop him.'

'You promised you'd look after it, Suzie.'

'I tried, Tom! I really did!'

'This is a disaster,' he said, as the full implication hit him. 'We spent a whole day putting that tape together and now it's gone.'

'I'm sorry, Tom. I feel terrible about it.'

'What use is that? We sweated blood to record those tracks. Do you know how much it costs to hire that studio? Do you know how long we've been waiting for this chance? And you've thrown it all away in a matter of seconds.'

'I didn't throw it away, Tom. I was mugged. You can get another made, surely?'

'Not at short notice,' he said. 'The studio's fully booked today. They can't break into someone else's recording time to run off a copy from our master tape. And I'm supposed to go round to the record company this afternoon. I need that tape – now!'

'Well,' said Suzie, grasping at straws, 'maybe it's been found and handed in at the police station by now.'

'I doubt that! The rest of the group will go bananas when they hear about this. Trudi will tear me apart.'

'But I was the one who lost the tape.'

'Yeah, but I was the one stupid enough to give it to you. I'm really sorry you got hurt but I can't forget this. It's ruined everything! I'm beginning to wish we'd never met!'

Suzie didn't hear the door slam behind him. She was too shocked. Tom had walked out of her life and she felt utterly destroyed. She was too stunned even to cry.

It was the last lecture of the afternoon at the medical school. The Professor of Anatomy was lecturing to a full theatre. Examinations were nearly on them and the students were feeling unprepared. They needed all the help they could get from their professors.

Gordy sat right at the back of the theatre so that he could keep an eye on Jo. Since their last conversation, he was steering well clear of her so that he didn't provoke another outburst. He was sitting several rows behind her. Like the other medical students, Gordy had listened intently to the lecture and made copious notes. But when he glanced down at Jo, she was sitting bolt upright, her arms stiffly by her side. It was very disturbing. Having borrowed her notes for lectures he'd missed in the past, he knew how assiduous she was in writing everything down. Why was she so detached from it all this time?

When the lecture was over, everyone gathered up their things and streamed out. Gordy lingered to watch her. Jo didn't move. She remained as stiff and motionless as a statue. Gordy was even more concerned. When the lecture theatre had emptied, he walked down the steps to join her.

'Jo,' he whispered.

There was no answer. She was staring straight ahead.

'It's me,' he said. 'Gordy.'

She still didn't answer. He sat down beside her.

'You know me, don't you, Jo?'

She looked at him, vaguely curious.

'No,' she said, quietly. 'I don't remember you.'

'I'm your friend. Gordy Robbins.'

'I don't think I've ever met you before.'

'Of course you have,' he continued. 'You've seen me every day this term.'

'Where?'

'Here – at the medical school.'

She jerked up in surprise. 'Medical school?'

'Don't you know where we are, Jo?' She shook her

head. 'Look around you, Jo. This is the lecture theatre. You've been here dozens of times. Surely you recognise it?'

'No,' she said, her eyes glazed and dull.

'Remember, we're first-year medical students.'

'Are we?'

'Yes, I'm Gordy Robbins and you're Joeline Barnes. See for yourself,' he said, pointing to the name on the front of her loose-leaf folder. 'Jo Barnes. That's you. Your name. In your own handwriting.'

She still looked uncomprehending.

'Of course you must know who you are.'

Her brow creased as she made an effort to concentrate but the dazed look stayed in her eyes. She shook her head and tried again. It was all in vain. She turned to Gordy with an expression of total bewilderment.

'Who did you say I am?' she asked.

'Jo Barnes.'

'And what am I doing here?'

'Don't you remember anything?'

'No,' she murmured. 'Nothing, nothing at all.'

Gordy's heart sank. Jo had finally cracked.

Chapter Ten

Bella was in a buoyant mood as she came out of the College of Nurses. Sister Killeen had actually praised her for once.

'You see?' said Mark. 'She does appreciate you.'

'At long last!'

'Sister Killeen picked you out from the whole year.'

'Yes,' said Bella, smoothing down her uniform. 'She was so amazed when I answered that question about hypoglycaemia. To be honest, I was amazed myself. I had no idea that I knew so much.'

'You'll make a good nurse one day.'

'That's what Sister Killeen said.'

They walked across the car park towards the main block. As they approached the Outpatients' Department, they saw a familiar figure. Suzie was standing tucked away in a recess. She still wore the sling and the bruises on her face had changed colour slightly. As people milled around the entrance to the building, she studied them carefully.

'What are you doing here?' asked Mark. 'You should be at home with your feet up.'

'Yes,' added Bella, 'who are you waiting for? Tom Peterson?'

'No, Bella. He's gone for good.'

'You mean you're not going to see each other again?'

'I'm afraid not.'

'That's incredible,' said Mark, looking quite shocked. 'I thought he'd be more understanding.'

'No,' sighed Suzie. 'All he could understand was that his demo tape was missing. Thanks to me.'

'It wasn't deliberate. You didn't ask to be mugged.'

'Did you explain the circumstances to Tom?'

'Yes. He was very sympathetic at first. But as soon as he realised his tape had gone as well, he got really upset. It was quite unpleasant, actually. He said he wished he'd never met me.'

'What a horrible way to treat you, especially as you've been hurt!' said Bella in disgust. 'He'd never pass the Sister Killeen Test for Nursing. Tom Peterson may look like a hunk but he's behaved like a slob.'

'It was very hurtful,' admitted Suzie. 'But not altogether a surprise. I mean, I did lose something that was entrusted to my care. That's why I'm here. Looking for him.'

'Who?'

'The mugger.'

'He won't come back,' said Mark.

'He might. The police said they usually have favourite patches. They think that the man who attacked me may be the same one who mugged a member of the clerical staff here. He probably hangs around the hospital.'

'Maybe. But he's hardly likely to come back the day after he's committed a crime here. That'd be sticking his neck out too far.'

'You never know.'

'Are you sure you'd recognise him again?' asked Bella.

'Oh, yes. I'll never forget that face.'

'He probably won't forget yours, either,' said Mark. 'If he sees you hanging around here, he won't come near the place. Even if he did, what could you do? I mean, you could hardly overpower him when your arm is in a sling.'

'I'd call Security.'

'Then the mugger would run a mile.'

'I've got to find him, Mark. I must get that tape back. It's the only way Tom will forgive me.'

'He doesn't deserve forgiveness,' said Bella, hotly. 'If I had his tape, I know where I'd put it! Tom Peterson would have to check into hospital to have it removed.'

'You're wasting your time, Suzie,' said Mark, kindly.

'Why not come back to the house with me?'

'But I'm sure it's worth a try,' said Suzie, looking desperate.

'Another day, perhaps. When you're feeling better. I'll stand out here with you then.' He put an arm round her. 'Come on.'

Suzie nodded and reluctantly allowed herself to be led away. Waiting for the mugger was a stupid gesture. He wouldn't return to the scene of the crime quite so soon. She could see that now.

Bella watched them go. After hearing about the way he'd treated Suzie, her interest in Tom had changed to fury. He was definitely off her list.

She saw Karlene walking towards her. 'Ready for action?' she asked.

'You bet! I'm in a mean mood, Karlene.'

'Then I'll let you punch it out with Mr Foss.'

'Right,' said Bella, grimly. 'I'll probably flatten him!'

Just at that moment, a deafening noise made them all jump out of their skins. The fire alarm had gone off again, this time inside the Outpatients' Department. The same wave of panic began and screams and cries of alarm could be heard as the swing doors were pushed open and outpatients tried to leave the building. Many had injuries which slowed them down and one – a boy with his leg in plaster – was carried out by his father. Everybody was badly jostled in the crowd and a few people were being knocked to the ground.

Mark and Suzie, hearing the noise, ran back and helped where they could but Bella was buffeted out of the way by the surge of frightened people. Out of the corner of her eye, she caught sight of a man letting himself out of a side door. Bella swung round to get a better look and saw that he was a Security guard. She was so enraged to see him leaving the scene of the crisis that she ran up to him.

'Hey! Where are you going? You're supposed to help.'

'I'm Security, not a fire officer,' he said.

'But you're supposed to be in there helping to calm people down,' she shouted.

'I'm going to get help!' he claimed.

'Well call for it on your mobile, then!' said Bella, angrily.

His hand automatically went up to the top pocket of his uniform but he wasn't carrying his mobile phone. Without a word of explanation, he ran off. Bella shouted after him. The panic had begun to ease but there was still a great deal of confusion inside the building.

Quite suddenly, the alarm went dead. No fire. For the third time a large number of vulnerable people had been scared out of their lives. The four friends were furious.

'Who keeps setting off the alarm?' asked Mark.

'It's such a stupid hoax,' said Bella.

'Stupid and dangerous,' added Suzie. 'Not only do people get injured in the rush but no one's going to trust that alarm any more. When we get a real fire, people won't believe it and they'll react too late. Someone's got to find out who's doing that.'

'We need more uniformed guards patrolling the hospital so that security is tightened and they can watch all the fire alarms in the building,' agreed Mark.

Bella was about to say something when she remembered the man who'd run out of the side door. He'd been in uniform but his presence in the Outpatients' Department hadn't stopped someone from setting off the alarm. Suspicion grew in her mind.

It took Gordy the best part of an hour to win Jo's trust. She finally accepted that something had caused her memory to fail. When she refused to go to her own doctor, Gordy persuaded her to have an informal chat with Damian Holt. As he was walking with Jo out of the medical school, she stopped dead in her tracks.

'Now I'm sure I've seen that before,' she said.

'That big building across the car park.'

'Of course you have,' Gordy assured her. 'That's the main hospital block. You walk past it every day.'

'I do?'

'Yes, Jo. Just take my word for it.'

'I suppose I'll have to... Gordy – that was your name, wasn't it?'

He nodded. 'Does any of this ring a bell?' he asked, as they walked towards the main gate. 'The Maternity Hospital, for instance?'

'Which one is that?'

'Over on the right.'

Jo stared at it for a moment then shook her head. Her eyes travelled to the next building and she nodded vigorously.

'I recognise that! I'm certain of it.'

'Do you know what it is?'

'The College of Nurses!'

'Well done!'

'If I remember that,' said Jo, taken aback, 'why can't I remember the Maternity Hospital?'

'Memory is very selective, I believe,' said Gordy.

'It's scary.'

'Hang in there,' he advised. 'You've already made some progress. An hour ago you didn't even know your name.'

'I'm Jo Barnes. At least I think I am.'

'No doubt about it. Let's go.'

Gordy led her through a corridor at the rear of the Casualty Department. He had arranged to meet Damian when his friend was off duty. They knocked on the door of Damian's office and he called them in.

Gordy introduced them. Jo was nervous but Damian smiled reassuringly.

'Good to meet you, Jo,' he said. 'Please, sit down.'

There were two chairs in the office and Damian took the chair behind his desk while Jo sat opposite him. Gordy hovered in the background. Damian was pleasant and relaxed.

'So,' he said, 'I hear you've been having a few problems with remembering things.'

'Yes,' said Jo. 'It does look that way.'

'Do you know who you are now, Jo?'

She nodded. 'Gordy told me,' she said. 'And there are things in my handbag with my name on.'

'When did this all start?' asked Damian.

'The night of the crash,' Gordy interrupted. 'Let me explain.' He gave Damian a brief account of what had happened and how Jo had reacted afterwards.

'Thanks, Gordy,' he said. 'Can you wait outside now, please. I'd like to have a chat with Jo, alone.'

'Can't I stay?'

'I know you're concerned, Gordy, but you'd only be in the way. You'll be a distraction – every time Jo struggles with an answer, you'll jump in with it. That wouldn't be any help. I need a few minutes on my own with her, OK?'

Gordy was disappointed. 'Fair enough,' he sighed.

'I'll send her out to you when we've finished,' said Damian. 'She'll find you. Jo may have forgotten everything else, but she'll remember you, Gordy!'

Bella favoured a full-blown attack but Karlene felt that a more tactful approach was needed. They were still debating strategy when they reached their landlord's house. When he came to the door, they could smell his cheap aftershave.

'Not you two again!' he moaned.

'Hello, Mr Foss,' said Karlene, brightly.

'You won't get rid of us so easily this time,' warned Bella.

'Ssh Bella! We've been looking at our rental agreement with you, Mr Foss.'

'That's funny,' he said. 'So have I. My obligations are clear. They're spelled out in black and white.'

'Yes,' agreed Karlene, taking out her copy of the contract. 'Clause Seven. The landlord is responsible for any repairs to the property that become necessary.'

'Go on then. Read the rest of it. You've missed the small print underneath, Karlene.'

She turned to the relevant page and scanned it with Bella. Alec Foss chuckled when he saw the consternation on their faces.

'Found it?' he taunted. 'Let me quote. "The repairs must be carried out within a calendar month of an inspection visit to the property by the landlord and a builder." What I don't see, I can't mend. That's my safety clause.'

'It's criminal!' shouted Bella.

'Then why did you sign the agreement?'

'Because we trusted you.'

'I've always had a kind face,' he smirked.

'Look, Mr Foss,' said Karlene, barely managing to keep her temper. 'This is an emergency. More water came through my ceiling yesterday. My things were soaked. I had to move in with Bella last night.'

'That won't hurt you.'

'It's an inconvenience,' said Bella. 'We pay for a separate room each and that's what we want. Karlene would need water wings to sleep in that bed of hers.'

'Don't exaggerate,' he said.

'Wait till you see it!'

'That may not be for some time, Bella. I'm a busy man. I've got property all over the city. I can't come running every time you get a minor problem.'

'Our roof has got a great big hole in it!' Bella was shouting now.

'So has my ceiling,' said Karlene, firmly. 'That room is not fit for human habitation. Don't you care about the state of your property?'

'Of course I do,' he said. 'When there's wanton damage by my tenants. If there's the tiniest scratch on the fixtures and fittings, I'll want to know why.'

'What about the missing slates?'

'Blimey!' he groaned, rolling his eyes. 'Next time I'm over that way, I'll take a look at that roof. Right? Will that shut you up?'

'No!' said Bella, losing all control. 'You're not going to get away with this, Mr Foss. This is your last warning. If you don't pay for those repairs, we'll take you to court.'

'Now, don't you start threatening me, girlie.'

'We could fine you for breach of contract.'

'You just try! It costs money to take someone to court. Then there'll be my costs to pay when you lose.'

'The law's on our side, Mr Foss,' said Karlene.

'Huh! It will be months before the case even comes to court. By that time you might not be living in my property.'

'Why not?' asked Bella.

'Because I might decide you're unsuitable tenants. Some landlords won't touch students with a bargepole and now I can see why. One headache after another.'

'But we've always paid our rent on time,' reminded Karlene.

'Which reminds me,' he said, sarcastically. 'I've kept it fairly low out of kindness to you.' Bella snorted. 'If you're demanding cash for repairs, I'd have to claw it back somehow. Pass on the message to the others, will you?'

'What message?' asked Bella.

'If you carry on pestering the life out of me, I won't just put the rent up, I'll double it!' He smirked again. 'Have a nice walk back.'

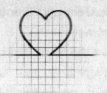

Chapter Eleven

Gordy leafed through a copy of his medical journal with growing irritation. He'd been sitting in the corridor outside Damian Holt's office for the best part of an hour. What was happening in there, and why wasn't he allowed to share in the consultation? He rolled up the magazine and stuffed it into his pocket before getting up. Just then the door opened. Damian came out into the corridor on his own and closed the door behind him.

'Well?' asked Gordy.

'She's got some problems, mate.'

'I know that. What can we do about them?'

'Strictly speaking,' advised Damian, 'she ought to go to her own GP. My guess is that he'd give her a referral to the psychiatric unit here.'

'I don't want her shunted off somewhere. Anyway, Jo won't go to her GP. It took me ages to convince her to chat to you. She knows you're a friend of mine.

That made you a lot less threatening to her.'

'I know. Look, Gordy, I think Jo is suffering from cumulative stress.'

'But Jo's always the least stressed person I know,' said Gordy, bewildered.

'That's only a front. Keeping it up has imposed additional huge stress on her. Jo's under terrific strain at the moment. I think she's finally reached a point where she can't cope any more and her systems have shut down.'

'You mean, her mind just went blank?'

'More or less,' said Damian, sighing. 'The only physical symptoms are signs of fatigue. She's obviously been pushing herself to the limit.'

'We've got exams next week. She's been working really hard. The strange thing is, she's the brightest student in our year, she could pass blindfold. But it's really unsettled her.'

'The exam's only one pressure. My guess is that there are others. Together, they've created an unbearable stress.' He looked at Gordy. 'Has she had any big emotional upset that you know about? Have you two split up or something? Any pregnancy fears?'

'Hang on! I'm not her boyfriend, if that's what you're thinking. We're just good mates. She doesn't have a regular boyfriend, she just wants to work and be one of the crowd.'

'There must be another source of stress, then. Has

there been a bereavement in her family? Any major changes in her life recently like moving house – anything?'

'Jo hasn't said anything to me.'

'What about her self-image – that can cause intense pressures in young women.'

'If there is a problem – she's kept it all to herself,' said Gordy.

'That's another primary cause of stress – keeping things secret from friends. Living with the fear that they may find out.'

'Find out what?' asked Gordy. 'That she's on drugs, steals things, what?'

'I'm just looking for possibilities,' said Damian, shaking his head. 'Her condition is quite worrying. Memory loss induced by high stress can be dangerous. We need to discover the underlying reasons for that stress.' He put a hand on Gordy's shoulder. 'That's where you come in, mate. She trusts you, Gordy. You may be able to discover what the root cause is.' He glanced at his office. 'Since I'm not her GP I can't really give her a prescription but I've recommended some pills she can buy over the counter. Mild tranquillisers. They'll relax her and help her to sleep.'

'Will she remember to take them, though?'

'Make sure she does.'

'I will, Damian. What else can I do to help?'

'Be very patient and understanding with her. Jo needs careful handling right now. Where does she live?'

'Quite close to me. She shares a flat with two other girls from our year. Kim and Yvonne.'

'This may take some time.'

'But will her memory come back?' asked Gordy, anxiously.

'Hopefully, yes. She's starting to remember some things already. That's a promising sign. Just let her go at her own pace.'

'Suppose none of this works?' asked Gordy.

'Then she should definitely see her GP and he will refer her to someone else within the hospital — probably the psychiatric department. Keep your fingers crossed. We might be able to avoid that. But she'll need a lot of support from her friends.'

'Thanks, Damian. You've been a great help.'

'That's OK.' He grinned suddenly. 'Hang on! Didn't you say one of her flatmates was called Yvonne? That couldn't be the same Yvonne you were crazy about not long ago, could it?'

Gordy looked embarrassed. 'No, no. I shouldn't think so,' he mumbled.

When the girls got back to the house, they were still fuming. Mark had to calm them down before he could get a rational explanation out of them. Then Bella and Karlene told him about their latest confrontation with the landlord.

'He can't double our rent!' protested Mark.

'Yes he can,' said Karlene. 'And he would.'

'But we took this house on a fixed rent. Mr Foss signed the agreement. He can't get out of that.'

'He can do what he likes,' said Bella vehemently. 'That contract's not worth the paper it's written on. If Karlene hadn't dragged me away, I'd have punched him on the nose!'

'What does he expect us to do? Pay for the repairs out of our own pockets?'

'Yes, Mark. We won't get a penny out of him.'

'We won't,' said Karlene. 'But Suzie might.'

'She's got other things on her mind at the moment,' said Mark. 'This business with Tom's really upset her.'

'Then we'll be doing her a favour by taking her mind off it,' said Bella. 'Where is she now?'

'Up in her room. She's resting.'

'Well, this is important.'

'Can't it wait, Bella?'

'No,' she insisted. 'It's waited too long already. Have you seen Karlene's room? It's like a lake.'

'I can't share with Bella indefinitely,' said Karlene.

'You could always have my room,' offered Mark. 'I could sleep down here on the sofa.'

'That's not the point. It's not fair on any of us,' said Bella. 'This is an emergency and we need to discuss it with Suzie. It concerns us all.'

'We just need her advice,' added Karlene.

Mark thought for a moment. 'You're right,' he said at length. 'She must be in on this. So should Gordy. We're all involved. I'll give her a call.' He went to the foot of the stairs. 'Suzie! Suzie! Can you come down for a minute?'

There was no response. He shrugged at the others.

'She can't hear you,' said Karlene. 'She's probably listening to a tape.'

'Country music,' decided Bella. 'It certainly won't be Stress. She'll never want to hear them again.'

Mark ran up the stairs and tapped on her door.

'Suzie! Are you in there, Suzie?'

There was no reply. He knocked harder, but there was still no answer. Mark felt worried and let himself in. The bedroom was empty. He checked the bathroom but that was empty as well. He ran down to the others.

'Suzie's not there,' he said. 'She must have slipped out when I wasn't looking. Where on earth could she have gone?'

Suzie finally found the right place. When she saw the van in the car park, she gasped with relief. Tom had told her that Stress rehearsed at a pub in Bessemer Road, but he'd forgotten to mention that the road was over a mile long. Suzie walked almost to the end of it before she spotted the van outside The White Lion.

She got close enough to hear the sound of Stress coming from an upstairs room but it was almost drowned out by the pulsing background music from the lounge bar. Suzie was too self-conscious to go into the pub on her own, so she lurked on the other side of the road. It was a long wait, on a dark evening, in a rough area of the city and she was frightened. Only her determination to see Tom kept her there.

Finally, the group came out of a back door. They loaded their instruments and equipment into the rear of the van then three of the girls went back into the pub but Trudi stayed to speak to Tom. Soon an argument developed and she started to gesticulate wildly. Before Tom could stop her, Trudi had swung round and marched back into the pub.

As Tom locked the rear doors of the van, Suzie came swiftly across the road. She had to seize her chance while she could.

'Tom!' she called, running across the car park.

'What are you doing here?' he said in surprise.

'I had to speak to you,' she gasped, panting.

'I'm not sure there's anything left to be said. Except that... Well, I'm sorry.'

'For what?'

'Going off the deep end like that.'

'I knew you'd be upset about the demo tape.'

'I overreacted, Suzie. You got mugged and all I could do was yell at you. I felt really terrible about it all afterwards.'

'Forget it,' she said, shrugging.

'It's just that so much was hanging on that tape.'

'I know.'

There was a pause. Suzie wasn't sure if they were friends again or not. Tom seemed uncertain about it.

'How are you, anyway?' he asked.

'I'll survive.'

'You got quite badly hurt, didn't you?'

'The police will get him sooner or later,' said Suzie, smiling.

'I hope they lock him up for a very long time.'

'I'd just like to get my things back.' She glanced at the pub. 'I heard you rehearsing up there.'

'Trying to rehearse,' he corrected. 'Trudi was being a right nuisance again. When she gets like that, it's useless. I've called it a day and they've all headed for the bar now. A drink or two might help a bit.'

'Is it because of me?'

'Partly,' he conceded.

'I'd do anything to get that tape back, Tom! Believe me!'

'It's too late,' he said. 'I had to tell the record

company that we hadn't got anything for them. They weren't too pleased, I can tell you.'

'Can't you get them to come and watch you play at a gig?'

'They've done that. Now they want to hear what we sound like on a record. But the studio can't run off another tape for two or three days, so the offer's not on the table any more.' He jerked a thumb at the pub. 'That's why Trudi's so hacked off. All that effort for nothing!'

'Make another tape!' urged Suzie. 'Can't you hire a different studio tomorrow? Put the same tracks on tape then rush it round to the record company. I caused this mess so I'll pay for the studio.'

'You don't understand. It costs an arm and a leg to do that.'

'I'll get the money from somewhere, Tom.'

'We'd never find a studio at such short notice.'

Suzie grabbed him impulsively with her good hand. 'There must be some way I can help!'

Tom was torn between affection and annoyance. He liked Suzie but he hadn't really got over what had happened. He tried to put it more gently this time.

'Let's just leave it for a while, Suzie. OK?'

Gordy felt pleased with the way Jo was responding. She seemed to have stabilised now. She was still very confused but she was beginning to recognise more and more things around her. They were enjoying a cup of tea in her flat. The familiar surroundings had given her memory a strong boost. She even remembered buying one of the posters on the wall.

'Look on the bright side,' he advised. 'You won't even have to sit that exam now.'

Jo looked bewildered and unsure for a moment.

'At the medical school, next week? Remember?' said Gordy.

'Oh, yes... I think I know about that.'

'There's no need. You've been excused on medical grounds. Damian has spoken to our professor and he's sending an explanatory letter. While the rest of us are sweating in that exam room, you'll be back here watching telly.'

'That's nice,' she said. But she didn't look as though she really meant it.

'Now, you must make sure you take those tablets.'

'I promise I will.'

'I'll stand over you until you do. And I must have a chat with Kim and Yvonne. Tell them what's happening. They're your friends, Jo, and that's who you need right now. I suppose the next thing will be to tell your parents.'

'My parents?'

'Yes. They'll want to know what's happened to you, Jo. Have you got their number? I could give them a ring.'

'My parents?' she repeated.

She looked blank, and Gordy jumped up and took down a framed photograph from the mantelpiece. It showed Jo and her parents on holiday in Crete. They were standing on a beach. Jo had shown it to Gordy a few weeks before.

'Here they are,' he said. 'Your parents.'

She took the photo and looked at it hard for a moment. Slowly recognition dawned. Suddenly, she pulled the photograph to her chest to hide it from him and stamped her foot.

'No!' she cried at the top of her voice. 'Don't you dare tell my parents! They mustn't know about me! They must never know!'

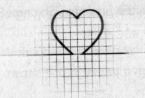

Chapter Twelve

Karlene was alone in the house when Suzie got back. She looked even more depressed than before. Karlene guided her gently to the sofa and sat her down.

'Where on earth have you been?' she asked.

'I went for a walk.'

'Do you know how late it is? Mark and Bella were so worried that they went out searching for you. The streets aren't safe at this time of night. You shouldn't be wandering around in that condition on your own.'

'I just needed some fresh air.'

Karlene wasn't fooled. She knew exactly where Suzie had been but there was no point in trying to make her say anything. Instead, Karlene made them both a cup of coffee and waited until Suzie had taken her first long sip.

'What did he say?' she asked.

'Who?'

'Tom. You went to see him, didn't you?'

Suzie gave up the pretence. She nodded sadly.

'Well?' prodded Karlene.

'They rehearse at a pub called The White Lion.'

'Was he pleased to see you?'

'Not really.'

'Then why bother with him, Suzie?'

'Because I feel guilty about what happened.'

'Tom's the one who should feel guilty. Getting so angry with you because his tape had been stolen. Couldn't he see the state you were in?'

'He apologised about that.'

'I should think so, too!'

'They were all counting on that demo tape, Karlene.'

'Then he shouldn't have let you borrow it, should he?'

'No,' conceded Suzie. 'But he did. That's what keeps coming back to me. I was special to him. Tom liked me enough to trust me with something as important as that.' She bit her lip. 'I miss him. I really want him to like me again.'

'Are you sure that he deserves you?'

'Look, we had something going between us.'

'But you hardly knew him, Suzie.'

'We just clicked. Don't ask me to explain it because I can't. All I know is that it's never happened before. This time, it did. Tom was wonderful to me.'

'Until you lost his tape.'

'I'll think of something,' vowed Suzie. 'I'm not going to let it come between us. Tom's worth fighting for and that's what I'm going to do!'

'I hope things work out for you, Suzie.'

'They've got to, Karlene.' She drank some more coffee and made an effort to brighten up. 'No more complaining. I won't bore you with my problems any more.'

'We've got enough of our own, as it happens. There's the small matter of the hole in the roof.'

'Didn't you report it to Mr Foss?'

'Twice,' said Karlene. 'Yesterday and today.'

'What was his reaction?'

'The first time he slammed the door in our faces. The second time he threatened to double our rent.'

'What?'

'For pestering him about it.'

'If there's a hole in the roof, the landlord has to mend it. No argument. It's there in the rental agreement.'

'So is the safety clause Old Fossie sneaked in. We took the contract with us, Suzie, but he just laughed in our faces. We thought we could force him to pay for the repairs but he just tied us in knots.'

'You should have let me go and see him.'

'We tried to. But you couldn't take it in then. You had other things on your mind.'

'Oh dear!'

'If you could just tell us how to deal with him…'

'I'll do better than that, Karlene,' promised Suzie. 'I'll call on Mr Foss myself. He usually listens to me in the end.' She held up her injured hand. 'I'll play on his sympathy. Maybe I should have a bandage around my head.'

'Throw in a limp as well. That should do the trick.'

'Just leave him to me!'

With the aid of his alarm clock, Mark was up early the next morning. After putting on his running gear, he crept quietly downstairs so that he wouldn't disturb the others. He was surprised to see a light on in the kitchen and even more surprised to see Gordy studying.

'What are you doing?' said Mark.

'Revising for my exam.'

'At this hour?'

'I have to catch up somehow,' explained Gordy. 'Jo's going to take up a lot of my time from now on. I didn't get back from her flat till after midnight.'

'How is she?'

'Not good, Marco. Apparently, everything got too much for her and she cracked under the strain.'

'Oh, no!'

Gordy gave him a detailed account of what had

happened and Mark was full of sympathy. He was also fascinated to hear about the tricks her memory was playing on her.

'Interesting, isn't it?' he observed. 'Jo has pushed all the nasty things out of her mind and only remembers the good things in her life.'

'She didn't remember me,' said Gordy, peevishly. 'And I'm the best friend she has.'

'You're her saviour. From the sound of it, you're doing a great job with her. But it's bound to make demands on your time.'

'And on my energy. I was quite tense and tired myself when I got back.'

'You look like death warmed up.'

'Thanks! You're a real friend!'

'Maybe you should join me for a run.'

'Don't be sadistic!'

'It might help to blow the cobwebs away, Gordy.'

'The cobwebs are the only things holding me together.'

Mark grinned and moved towards the door. He turned back again as a thought struck him. 'That business about her parents,' he said. 'That's really strange.'

'It frightened the life out of me.'

'It could mean something important.'

'I'm sure it does.'

'Did you ask her why she reacted like that?'

'I didn't dare to, Marco. She's too volatile at the moment. She might have done anything.'

'But she recognised them. That's a promising sign. What did her flatmates say about her parents?'

'I didn't get a chance to ask them. It wasn't a subject I could talk about when Jo was still within earshot. Besides, Kim and Yvonne had enough to do when they learnt what had happened to Jo. They were trying to take it all in themselves.'

'Did Jo recognise them?'

'Eventually she did.'

'So you did make some progress?'

'Having her flatmates there helped. Kim and Yvonne are great. They couldn't have been more supportive.'

Mark smiled. 'Is that the Yvonne you used to fancy?'

'Don't bring that up, please,' he groaned.

'It is, isn't it? She came to a party here.'

'Time for your run, Marco.'

'Yvonne. That's right. You really fell for her. Yvonne was the one who—'

'That's enough,' said Gordy through gritted teeth. 'There are some things I don't want to remember, Marco, and she is one of them. Yvonne's being great with Jo at the moment and that's all I care about.'

Bella climbed gingerly into the loft with a torch. Karlene followed her up the ladder and put her head through the trap door.

'The pans are over to the left, Bella.'

'Oh yes. There they are.'

'Is there much water in them?'

'Quite a bit,' said Bella. 'We must've had more rain in the night.' She yelped as she banged her head on a rafter. 'We need a proper light up here.'

'And a proper roof.'

'Have you got the bucket ready?'

'Yes,' said Karlene. 'Pass the pans over and I'll empty them. Be quick. It's cold up here.'

They were inspecting the pans before leaving for the hospital. It was a boring job but it had to be done. When the bucket was full, Karlene took it into the bathroom to pour down the sink. She could hear Bella moving about.

'What are you doing?' she called.

'Taking a closer look at your ceiling.'

'It looks worse from below,' said Karlene, going into her own room. 'The plaster has come down in two places.'

'It's still soaking wet up here, too.'

'I hate that smell of damp.'

'I'll just crawl to the far end.'

'Be careful, Bella. Stay on the joists.'

'I know what I'm doing, don't worry.'

'Watch out for those nails in the rafters.'

Karlene looked up with trepidation. There were thumping noises from above, then an eerie silence. It was soon shattered by a scream from Bella and one foot came crashing through the ceiling, then another, then her whole body. She fell onto the mattress below in a snowstorm of plaster dust.

'Are you all right?' asked Karlene, coughing.

'Something attacked me,' gasped Bella.

They both looked up at the gaping hole in the ceiling. A large moth came through it and circled the room. When they realised that Bella's attacker was a harmless moth, they burst out laughing.

Karlene looked around the debris in her room.

'One more item on the landlord's bill,' she said, cheerfully. 'Suzie will make him cough up.'

It was another long and frustrating day at the hospital. Suzie's broken fingers still throbbed and the bruises on her face attracted several unwanted stares. She concentrated hard on her work and Geraldine Hobson was pleased with her. But the hours seemed to pass very slowly. Tom was never far from her mind and she clung to the hope that he might ring. But he didn't.

At the end of the day, she left the hospital by the exit close to where she was mugged. She spent a few fruitless minutes looking around for the young man who'd attacked her – then gave up. The mugger might never come back there again. Right now, something else needed her attention. She had to confront the landlord.

'Blimey!' he said, gaping at her. 'What happened to you, Suzie?'

'I was mugged outside the hospital.'

'You look as if you've been three rounds with Frank Bruno. What did they take?'

'My handbag. When I fought back, he punched me. My fingers got broken.'

'Nowhere's safe these days,' grumbled the landlord. 'Come on in a minute. You need a sit down.'

His sympathy was genuine. He took her into a large living room with a floral carpet and a suite in bright red leather. She perched on the edge of the sofa. Suzie decided on a different tack.

'I'm sorry if my friends bothered you, Mr Foss.'

'They were a pesky nuisance, those two.'

'They were just trying to do what they thought was right.'

'I don't ever want to see their faces here again!'

'That's why I've come this time.'

'Good. I can do without them.'

'Karlene's the one who's really suffered. Her room looks as if a bomb's hit it.'

'That's not my fault.'

136

'No, Mr Foss,' she said, calmly. 'But it does mean that we're paying for five bedrooms and only using four. So we expect to pay less rent at the end of the month.'

'Now, hang on a minute.'

'That was the agreement. A room each.'

'I go by numbers. Five tenants means full rent, even if you all sleep in the same room.'

'Now you know that's not fair.'

'It's the way I work, Suzie. Like it or lump it.'

'That roof is in a bad state, Mr Foss.'

'Then get it repaired.'

'If we do, we'll send you the bill.'

'Fine,' he said, airily. 'It'll go straight in the bin.'

'That roof is your responsibility and you know that really,' Suzie was determined to press her point.

'All I'm liable for is necessary repairs and I don't believe that they are necessary – yet. Tell you what I'll do, Suzie,' he said, easing her out of the chair. 'When I get a chance, I'll drive round to the property and take a look myself. OK? It may not be for some while, mind, because I've got a lot on at the moment. You know how it is. So bear with me, eh?' His voice darkened. 'And keep those two friends of yours off my back.'

Suzie found herself back in the drive.

'Those repairs are essential,' she said. 'We want action now.'

'You're on my list, Suzie. Thanks for calling.'

He waved her away and went back into the house. Suzie felt wretched. She had achieved nothing. And Karlene and Bella had put their faith in her. Now Suzie would have to admit that she'd failed miserably.

Chapter Thirteen

Gordy's patience was being tested to the limit. He was taking Jo on a tour of the medical school to see if it triggered any memories for her. Opening a door, he guided her through it.

'Where are we now? Do you recognise this place?' he said.

'It's a library.'

'Yes, that's right, Jo. But what library?'

'I-I don't think I know.'

'Try again,' he coaxed.

'I don't think I've ever seen it before.'

'Over there,' he said, pointing. 'By the window. That was your favourite seat. Do you remember sitting there? Think hard, Jo.'

'I'm trying to, Gordy.'

'Is there anything here that you recognise?'

'It's all a blur. I have faint memories, that's all.'

'What about the librarian?' he asked, indicating the

chubby woman who sat behind the main desk. 'Surely you remember Mrs Rogers?'

Jo looked closely at her. 'Vaguely,' she said doubtfully.

Gordy sighed as he brought her out of the library. 'Let's try the lecture theatre,' he said.

It was hard work. Gordy had convinced Jo that she was a first-year medical student at the hospital and she was eager to be shown around, but the results were disappointing. Jo recognised a few things but most were completely unfamiliar to her. She was still trapped in her own private world; still confused and bewildered.

Gordy resolved to stay positive. There had been some improvement. The tablets from the chemist had ensured a good night's rest and Jo seemed more relaxed. Some signs of her stress had disappeared and Kim and Yvonne, her two flatmates, had helped her enormously. The slow process of unlocking her thoughts had begun, but Gordy knew the precarious state of Jo's mind and that he had to go very easily or he might tip her over the edge.

The lecture theatre was empty when they arrived. Jo gazed around it like a stranger. She shook her head.

'N-no, I don't think so.'

'You were in here almost every day,' Gordy reminded her, gently. 'Look around carefully. Is there anything that rings a bell?'

'I wish there was.' Her eyes roamed around the room again, then settled on the dais at the front. 'Yes,' she said, firmly. 'I've seen that before. I seem to remember a tall man with silver-grey hair and a goatee beard.'

'Gilbert Buchanan!'

'I can remember him standing right there!' Her face lit up.

'He often lectured to us in here and he was the one who gave that Memorial Lecture at St Catherine's Hospital.'

'A blue suit with a red carnation in the buttonhole.'

'That's him.'

'It's all coming back now.'

'Good girl, Jo! Keep it up. You're winning.'

Gordy felt much happier as he led her out of the room. Students were trickling towards them on their way to a lecture. One of them was Jo's flatmate, Yvonne, a tall, willowy girl with fair hair. Gordy had been really keen on her but their romance had never got off the ground. So he was surprised when she gave him such a friendly smile.

'Hi, Gordy!'

'Oh. Hi, Yvonne.'

'Hello, Jo.'

'Hello…' said Jo, tentatively. For a moment she looked dazed again. Then she said, 'That's right. Yvonne and Kim. I remember. Kim is the one with the ponytail. You're Yvonne.' She looked relieved.

'How's it going?' asked Yvonne.

'Pretty good, I think,' said Gordy. 'Slow but sure.'

'Great. I think you're being really supportive, Gordy.'

She put her hand on his arm briefly before going into the lecture theatre. Gordy grinned with pleasure. Helping Jo might have an unexpected bonus.

'She likes you,' said Jo, smiling.

Gordy led her towards the laboratories, nodding hello to other students who passed them. They smiled at Jo, too, but she clearly didn't recognise them. Suddenly, she stopped in the corridor.

'I feel I've been here before,' she announced.

'You have, you're right.'

'It's nothing specific but this atmosphere is very familiar. I feel comfortable in it. At home. I like it here, Gordy.'

'That's true – you love it. Can you remember what made you want to become a doctor in the first place?'

'I don't know, I'm not sure. No, that's too difficult. I can't remember.'

'I'm sure you can, if you try,' he urged. 'You remembered Gilbert Buchanan. I'm sure you can remember this as well.' He smiled encouragingly. 'Now, think. What first made you want to be Doctor Barnes?'

'Doctor Barnes?' she echoed. Jo seemed to stagger for a moment, as if hit by some terrible blow. Her eyes rolled, her face went white and her jaw tensed. She began to sway on her feet. As Gordy reached out to steady her, she pushed him away and lurched off down the corridor.

'You really don't need to come with me, Mark,' said Suzie.

'Well, I'm going to anyway.'

'I'll be fine on my own.'

'Don't argue, Suzie. There'll be a big crowd there. The last thing you want is someone bumping into your injured hand. I can protect you, be your bodyguard. Anyway,' he added, 'I'm the one who found out that Stress were playing tonight. And I want to hear them again, too – I like their sound.'

Mark had seen the poster on the noticeboard at the College of Nurses. A gig was being held at the University and Stress were supporting the rock band who were the main attraction. Suzie was hurt that Tom hadn't mentioned it to her, but she was glad that she wasn't going to miss it. They decided to walk the half-mile to the University.

'I shouldn't have let Mr Foss trick me like that,' she said, still feeling despondent about her meeting with him. 'I should have pressed him much harder.'

'He's a slippery customer, Suzie.'

'I know, but I've always managed to deal with him in the past. Not this time. He ran rings round me. I'm just not up to it, Mark.'

'That's understandable. None of us think you've let us down.'

'I feel bad about Karlene, especially. Her room's in chaos.'

'Bella did her share towards that,' noted Mark with a grin. 'She brought down most of the ceiling.'

'That's because it was soaked through.'

'And the moth was partly to blame.'

'There has to be a way to make Mr Foss pay for the repairs. There just has to be, Mark.'

'We'll find one, don't worry.'

They turned in through the gates of the University. It had begun life as a technical college. Now it had full university status, but it still had the same old redbrick buildings. The gig was being held in a huge cellar, which had been fitted out with strobe lights. It was already packed with students and Suzie and Mark had to stand at the back. As she was nudged and jostled, Suzie was glad that Mark was with her.

Stress were on first but they gave a tired performance. Tom sang without any real feeling and the rest of the group seemed listless. When they'd finished their set, it felt as though the crowd gave them more applause than they deserved, but the real cheers were reserved for the rock band who came on after them. Mark and Suzie moved towards the exit.

'I must see Tom again,' she said in Mark's ear, trying to make herself heard above the noise.

'Do you think that's a good idea?'

'I want to. I really want to, Mark.'

'But what will he feel, Suzie?' he said, gently. 'I'd hate you to get hurt again. Maybe the best thing is to let things ride for a while. Contact him in a week or so – he may feel differently by then.'

But Suzie was convinced she wanted to speak to him. They waited outside until the group appeared and started to put their gear in the van. The four girls went back into the building while Tom locked up the vehicle. Suzie took a deep breath and went up to him.

'Oh hi, Suzie,' he said, smiling at her. 'I didn't expect to see you here.'

'You were great tonight,' she said.

'We were lousy and you know it.'

'Come on, it wasn't as bad as that.'

'Then where are the fans?' he said, looking around. 'I don't see any. We went down like a lead balloon.'

'Well, Mark and I are here, two of your greatest fans.' Tom looked slightly embarrassed. There was an awkward pause and then he looked at her bruises.

'How are you feeling now?'

'Better, thanks.'

'Have the police found out who mugged you?'

'No, not yet.'

'I hope they do,' said Tom with feeling.

'Me too.' Suzie went closer to him. 'I meant what I said yesterday, Tom, about paying for another recording session.'

'No chance!' he said.

'Have they run off another tape at Nirvana Studio?'

He hunched his shoulders. 'That's a sore point.'

'Why don't they just give you the master tape?'

'It's to do with their insurance policy. We haven't paid the full amount for the hire of the studio yet,' he explained. 'That's why we're doing every gig we can. Until we clear our debt, Nirvana won't release the master tape or run off another copy.'

'But that's blackmail!'

'It's business, Suzie. We owe them money.'

'They'll get it,' she said. 'Why don't I pay the rest of the money then you can claim the tape? I'll write you a cheque.' She suddenly froze. 'Oh, no! How stupid! My cheque book was in the handbag that was stolen.'

'You couldn't afford to settle our debt, anyway. We owe about eight hundred quid.'

'As much as that?' she gasped.

'And we wouldn't take your cash, in any case. Stress will sort it out somehow. Forget the whole thing.'

'I can't, I've spoiled your chance of a recording contract.'

'Look,' he said. 'That's why we should… keep out of each other's way.'

'But I want to see you, Tom.'

She touched his arm and he smiled. But before he could speak, a figure came rushing out of the building. Trudi put her arm through Tom's and drew him away.

'Come on, love,' she said. 'We need you in there.'

She gave Suzie a dismissive nod, then she and Tom vanished through a door. Suzie felt rejected and embarrassed. Mark came across to join her.

'Time to go home?' he said, quietly.

♡

They met in a bar close to the hospital. Gordy was still so upset about everything that had happened, that he couldn't even feel much pleasure about the thought of a drink alone with Yvonne. In any case, it wasn't really a date. They were meeting to discuss Jo.

'Is she more relaxed now?' asked Gordy.

'Yes. We've been reminding her to take the pills.'

'I was alarmed when she went charging off like that in the medical school. I thought she might do something nasty to herself. I was so relieved when I caught up with her.'

'Don't blame yourself, Gordy.'

'But I seemed to trigger something off.'

'Unintentionally. She realises you're a friend – in fact you're more than that,' said Yvonne. 'Without your support, Jo would have really gone to pieces. They'd probably have had to admit her to the psychiatric wing.'

'That's where I'll end up as well, probably!' said Gordy, trying to make a joke of things. He pulled such a crazy face that Yvonne started to laugh.

She looked serious again as she said, 'There are bound to be setbacks, Gordy. These things don't get better quickly, you know.'

'That wasn't just a setback,' said Gordy, sadly. 'It was a near disaster. I hadn't realised how fragile she was. Jo actually seemed to be recovering.'

'She'll recover again. When she settles down.'

'Where is she now?'

'She's with Kim.'

'Has Jo mentioned my name at all?'

'No. She's hardly said anything.'

'I'm sure that's a bad sign.' He shook his head. 'If only I knew what had provoked that reaction. It's baffling! One minute we're the best of friends and the next minute, she can't get away from me quickly enough.'

'What were you talking about?'

'Medicine, I think.'

'Go on.'

'I just asked her why she wanted to be a doctor.

That was all. It seemed a simple question that might connect her with her life again. I actually said, "What made you want to become Doctor Barnes?"'

'Were those your exact words?'

'More or less.'

'You actually said "Doctor Barnes" to her?'

'Yes. What was wrong with that?'

Yvonne finished her drink and looked at him solemnly.

'I think I can guess,' she said.

Chapter Fourteen

Bella first heard the noise in the middle of the night. It was a distant fluttering. She thought that the wind might be making her curtains flap but the window was shut. Karlene wasn't disturbed by the sound at all. She lay snoring quietly on the floor beside the bed. Bella slowly drifted off to sleep again.

The alarm clock went off in the next room. Mark killed its distinctive ping at once, but not before it had roused Bella. Once again, she heard the fluttering noise. It was much louder this time and seemed to be coming from outside. Clambering out of bed, she reached for her dressing gown and stepped over Karlene's prone body on the floor. When she went out into the passageway, she realised that the sound was coming from Karlene's room. She opened the door and peered in.

The noise stopped instantly. Bella switched on the light and reeled backwards from the scene of devastation. There were chunks of fallen plaster everywhere and a film of dust lay over the whole room. But there was nothing to explain the strange fluttering sound. She was about to shut the door again when she glanced up at the hole in the ceiling.

Suddenly, something came dive-bombing down towards her and sent her cowering against the wall in terror. When it brushed against her hair, she dropped to a crouching position with her arms up to shield her head. The fluttering seemed to fill the whole room. Too frightened to move or call out, Bella kept her eyes tightly shut. It seemed to go on for ever but at last Mark appeared.

'What's that noise?' he asked.

'Help,' she whispered. 'Help me, Mark.'

He saw the problem at once. A bird was circling the room at speed. When it tried to fly out of the window, it banged against the glass, sending itself into a complete frenzy. It flapped its wings madly against the curtains.

'Mark, what's happening?' asked Bella, still too terrified to look up.

'Don't worry,' he said. 'I can handle this. No problem.'

He lifted up the sash window and the bird flew gratefully out. Mark knelt down beside Bella. 'You can open your eyes now. The bird's gone.'

'Bird?' She lowered her arms. 'Is that what it was?'

'Just a sparrow.'

'It seemed much larger. Like a vulture.'

'No, Bella,' he said, helping her up. 'It was only a sparrow. It must have come through the hole in the roof and couldn't find its way out again.'

'This is dreadful,' she complained. 'Yesterday, a moth attacked me. Today it's a sparrow. Tomorrow it'll be a golden eagle. By the end of the week, Concorde will be flying in.'

'That'll be worth seeing!' said Mark, laughing.

'It's not funny. This can't go on.'

'I know. Suzie and I had a long talk about it.'

'What are you going to do?'

'Try a different approach to our landlord.'

She looked anxiously up at the hole in the ceiling.

'Are you sure it was only a sparrow?'

'No,' he said. 'It was a giant condor!'

This time they both laughed.

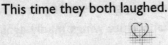

Suzie examined her face in the mirror. The bruises were definitely fading. With careful make-up, she would be able to hide most of them. Being able to use only one hand slowed her down, but she persevered. When she finally came down for breakfast, Suzie found Karlene making toast in the kitchen. Her friend looked up at her with an approving grin.

'Wow! You look almost normal again, Suzie!'

'Thanks.'

'Did you sleep well?'

'Until I rolled over onto my injured hand. That really hurt.'

'You'll be able to compare your bad night with Bella, then.'

'Why? What happened?'

'Bella's version is that she was trapped in my room with a flock of attacking seagulls — just like that film, you know — The Birds. Mark reckons that one tiny sparrow flew in through the roof. I believe him.'

'So do I. Is he out running again?'

'Yes. He's really taking this marathon seriously.'

'He must be pretty fit by now.'

The toast popped up from the machine and Karlene put it into a rack and set it on the table in front of Suzie.

'Help yourself. There's coffee in the pot.'

'Thanks.'

'Mark says you've had a brainwave about the repairs.'

'Fresh tactics, that's all. But don't get too excited. They may not work.'

'What are we going to do to Mr Foss?'

'Do you mind if I wait until the others are here?' said Suzie. 'All five of us need to be in on it. Mark already knows but Bella won't want to be left out. Nor will Gordy.'

'He'll have to be, he's already gone. He left at the crack of dawn.'

'Gordy's gone to the medical school this early?'

'No, Suzie. He's gone to Birmingham. Jo Barnes comes from Birmingham and Gordy's gone to see her parents. It's something to do with her father, I think.'

'Jo's father?'

'Yes,' said Karlene. 'Doctor Barnes.'

It was a long and expensive journey but Gordy kept telling himself that it would be worthwhile. Damian had told him they must try and find the root causes of Jo's stress, then they could start to unravel her confused mind and help her on the road to recovery. After talking with Yvonne at the bar, Gordy decided that a visit to Birmingham was essential though he wasn't at all certain what he would find there.

The house was in Edgbaston, close to the cricket ground – Gordy had seen test matches from there on television. It was a double-fronted Victorian property with three storeys and it was obviously well cared for. When he saw the gleaming car on the drive, Gordy wondered how Jo's parents would react when he told them about the way she'd crashed his ancient Astra.

At the last moment, he'd had second thoughts. Coming to Jo's home behind her back seemed like a betrayal. Twice when he'd mentioned her family, Jo had reacted wildly. If she knew what he was doing now, she might become even more hysterical. Gordy considered turning round and going straight back home.

But he decided to stick to his original plan. Having come all this way, it would be foolish not to contact her parents. They had a right to know their daughter was so ill and Gordy was sure they would handle the situation sensitively.

When he pressed the bell, it chimed deep inside the house. A woman answered the door. She looked elegant and was wearing an expensive suit; her hair was shining and well-groomed – but she looked too young to be Jo's mother. Gordy cleared his throat.

'Mrs Barnes?'

'No. Do you want Doctor Barnes?' she asked. 'Because I'm afraid he's at morning surgery. He won't be back until lunchtime. Can I take a message?'

'I need to speak to him about his daughter, Jo. My name's Gordy Robbins. I'm a friend of hers – we're in the same year at medical school.'

'Is there something wrong?'

'Yes, I'm afraid so.'

'Oh dear!' said the woman, alarmed. 'Has she been in an accident?'

'Well, there was an accident,' he explained. 'In my car. But neither of us was injured. No, it's something else. It's rather complicated. Is there any way I could speak to Doctor Barnes now?'

'Surgery doesn't finish until one – sometimes later.'

'What about her mother? When will she be back?'

'I'm sorry,' she said. 'Mrs Barnes doesn't live here any more.'

Reg Beazely was a short, fat, slovenly old man in a flat cap and a pair of dungarees. He had a habit of smoking his cigarettes to the bitter end, and had a disconcerting way of talking to himself – but he obviously knew his job. Mark had given up his lunch hour to show the builder round the house and it proved to be an education.

'How did you find me?' asked Beazely.

'In the Yellow Pages.'

'Well, you picked the right man for the job, son.'

'We just need an estimate at this stage.'

'Estimates are free. Courtesy guaranteed.' He touched his cap deferentially, dragging on his cigarette. Then he started talking to himself.

'Nice house,' he said. 'Badly neglected. Look at that rot. Smell that damp. Fading paintwork. No undercoat. Shouldn't be allowed. And all that perished brickwork outside.'

'The real problem's upstairs,' said Mark, not wanting him to be deflected from the real problem.

'Quite a few down here as well, son.'

'Could you make a note of everything, please?'

Still chatting to himself, the builder wrote something in the large pad he was carrying. Then he followed Mark up to Karlene's room. Reg chuckled.

'There's more holes than ceiling up there.'

'How much will it cost to repair?'

'Don't rush me, son. I'm looking. Got to decide if it's worth patching up or quicker to pull the rest down and give you a new ceiling. Yes, you see? Six sheets of plasterboard would just about do it. Bit of a boozer, eh, the person who sleeps here?'

'Boozer?' Mark was bewildered.

'She woke up plastered! Get it?'

Beazely chuckled at his own joke then scribbled in his pad. Mark left him to it. The builder went up into the loft then took a ladder from the top of his van so that he could inspect the roof from outside. He was slow but thorough. When he'd finished, he'd covered four pages of his notebook.

'This'll cost you a pretty penny, son,' he said.

'We're trying to make the landlord pay.'

'And who might that be?'

'He's called Mr Foss.'

'What? Old Alec Foss? Bald geezer with a tash?'

'That's him.'

'Right old skinflint, he is.'

'You can say that again,' said Mark desperately.

'If you show him this estimate, he'll run a mile. No,

there's only one way to get a crook like Alec to cough up.'

'What's that, Mr Beazely?'

'Look, son, I'll tell you if you really want me to.'

Mark nodded enthusiastically. They might yet get their revenge.

♡

Determined to put her problems behind her, Suzie concentrated on her studies all morning and Geraldine Hobson was very pleased with her. As she headed for the canteen at lunchtime, her thoughts turned to Gordy. She wondered how he was getting on in Birmingham. His commitment impressed her. Gordy was sometimes a figure of fun in their household but she knew that he could be relied on in a crisis. And it looked as though he would go to any lengths to help Jo. She really was in a state. Two broken fingers couldn't begin to compare with Jo's total loss of memory and identity. Suzie would never feel sorry for herself again.

Nearing the canteen, she was greeted by a warm smile. Tom was lounging outside the door.

'What took you so long?' he said.

'Tom!'

'You told me you always lunched in the canteen.'

'I do,' she said, feeling quite shaken at seeing him. 'Look, I'd ask you in but it's staff only, I'm afraid.'

'I can't stay, anyway. I just wanted a quick word. Look Suzie, about last night.'

'I shouldn't have come.'

'Of course you should. It was a public performance.' He made a face. 'We were rubbish. You should have asked for your money back.'

'It's true, I have heard you play better, Tom.'

'I hope you will again some time.'

'Yes,' she said. 'But I shouldn't have hung about afterwards trying to see you,' she said honestly.

'I was pleased to see you.'

'Trudi wasn't. I guessed there was something between you two.'

'That's what I came to explain. Trudi was out of order last night, dragging me off like that. And I shouldn't have let her do it, either.'

'She's part of your group, and she's entitled to feel like that.'

'In some ways, yes.'

'Look, I won't try and see you again, Tom,' she promised. 'Now I know you've got a girlfriend, I'll stay out of your way.'

'Girlfriend?' said Tom, surprised.

'Yes, Trudi. Your drummer.'

'She's not my girlfriend, Suzie. The only reason she pulled me away last night was because she thought you were just another groupie trying to move in on me. And she was still fed up about the tape. Trudi's my protector. When the fans get too crazy, she comes to my rescue.' He grinned.

'But you seem really close.'

'We are,' he said. 'I thought you knew. Trudi's my sister, not my girlfriend.'

Bella was halfway down the stairs when she saw him. The security guard was going through the door that led to the second floor. There was something familiar about him but she couldn't put her finger on it. The reassuring thing was that he was patrolling the building. Since the false alarms, security had been made more visible. It made everyone at the hospital feel a lot safer.

Suddenly, there was an eruption of noise. The fire alarm was the loudest yet, echoing through the main block and spreading chaos everywhere. Bella's instinct was to get downstairs as fast as she could but she suddenly remembered what was odd about the security guard. It must be the same man she'd seen leaving the Outpatients' Department.

Bella felt a surge of anger. She pushed open the door to the second floor and sprinted along the corridor, dodging the nurses who were rushing to their wards. As she turned a corner into another corridor, she was just in time to see the security man slipping into the Gents. It was obviously his hiding place. He would wait in there while the hospital was in a state of panic and confusion. It was the last place anyone would search for him.

People were everywhere now, rushing down the corridor towards her and cries could be heard all around the building. Bella shouted at the top of her voice.

'False alarm! It's another false alarm!'

But the terrifying noise of the bell drowned her out. This was the fourth time that this unnecessary panic had been created in the hospital. It was cruel and dangerous. Bella became suddenly determined that it would never happen again if she had anything to do with it. Grabbing a trolley, she wheeled it against the door of the Gents then piled it high with every chair she could lay her hands on. Her anger gave her strength. She even managed to drag a bedside cabinet out of a nearby ward to reinforce her barricade. Then she turned a second trolley sideways so that it was jammed between the toilet and the wall. He wouldn't escape now.

When the alarm finally stopped, Arthur Garrett, the Head of Security, came pounding down the corridor with four of his men. He and Bella had met before, though not in circumstances like this. What was she doing outside the Gents?

'He's in here, Mr Garrett!' she shouted as he approached. 'That man who set off the fire alarm.'

'You saw him do it?'

'Yes,' she said. 'Here and in the Outpatients' Department. He's one of your own men.'

'Never!' he said, angrily. 'I keep good discipline here.'

'But I know it's him because he doesn't have a mobile phone in his top pocket like the rest of you. He's just wearing the uniform. And his behaviour's been so fishy when the alarms have gone off.'

Arthur Garrett looked knowingly at his men.

'I bet it's Bill Phelps,' he said, grimly. 'I sacked him a week ago for idleness. He said he'd get his own back.' He turned to his men. 'Right lads, dig him out of the toilet and drag him along to my office. I'd like a private word with Bill Phelps before I hand him over to the police.'

'I knew it was him!' cried Bella, triumphantly.

'Well done, girl!' said Arthur. 'You deserve a medal for this, Bella. I'll tell that Sister Killeen of yours, too.'

'Thanks, Mr Garrett.'

'People will think twice about setting off a fire alarm now.' He glanced at the barricade that his men were slowly dismantling. 'And I'll think twice about going to the Gents while you're around.' And he winked at her.

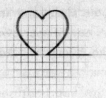

Chapter Fifteen

It was nearly two o'clock when Doctor Geoffrey Barnes returned from his morning surgery. He was surprised when he saw Gordy on the sofa, drinking what was his third cup of tea. But surprise turned to concern when he heard why Gordy had come.

'What's wrong with Jo?' he asked urgently.

'My mate, Doctor Damian Holt, at the hospital, called it cumulative stress.'

'What are her symptoms?' It was though the doctor part of him had taken over.

'A nervous breakdown, more or less. Jo's mind seemed to blank out. She didn't appear to know who she was, or what she was doing in medical school. It was quite scary, doctor.'

'Listen, Gordy, could you be a bit more specific, please? Were there any warning signs? How's her health generally?'

Gordy was about to launch into a full explanation

when he saw the woman hovering near the door. He'd already worked out that she was sharing the house with Jo's father. She looked very much part of the place and talked about Doctor Barnes with a possessive tone and a warmth that gave away their relationship.

'Could you give us a few minutes alone, Wendy?' asked the doctor.

'But I want to know what's happened, Geoffrey.'

'I'll tell you later. But I'd really rather hear Gordy's story on my own, if that's OK, Wendy.' He looked concerned and slightly irritated. 'Jo is my daughter.'

Wendy nodded. 'I'll be in the kitchen if you want me,' she said, obviously hurt by being excluded. 'Don't be too long.'

'Now, Gordy,' urged the doctor. 'Tell me everything you can.'

It was more of a medical consultation than a chat. Doctor Barnes asked the most searching questions about Jo's behaviour over the last couple of months and he seemed particularly keen to know the name of the tablets that Damian had recommended. Though he clearly loved his daughter, he spoke of her in the same detached manner he might discuss a patient.

'Has she responded in any way?' he asked Gordy now.

'Yes, Doctor Barnes. She remembers some things.'

'Can you give me an example?'

Gordy told him everything. It was only when he mentioned the incident outside the laboratory that he saw Jo's father flinch. It was when Gordy told him about how he used the words 'Doctor Barnes' and how that had really distressed her. Now he began to see why. She'd been proudly following in her father's footsteps when there was a major change in things at her home. A younger woman had moved in with her father. Maybe Jo could no longer respect him in the same way.

'It was good of you to come, Gordy,' he said.

'I really wanted to come – I felt her parents should know.'

'Thank you, I appreciate that.'

'Don't tell Jo, will you? About this visit, I mean.'

'Not if it will upset her unnecessarily. You've been extremely helpful but, if you don't mind, I think I'd like to speak directly to your friend, Doctor Holt.'

'I'll give you Damian's number at the hospital.'

'Good.'

'Is there any advice you can give us?' asked Gordy. 'About dealing with Jo, I mean. We're all a bit in the dark, really.'

'Let me speak to Doctor Holt first, then I'll tell you what I think we should do.'

'One other thing,' said Gordy, bravely. 'Shouldn't Mrs Barnes be told what's going on?'

'I'll tell her,' he said, crisply.

'Do you think I could speak to her myself? I'm sure she'd want to hear it directly from me, as I'm such a close friend of Jo's.'

Geoffrey Barnes was about to speak when he realised that Wendy had appeared in the doorway again, listening to every word. He looked embarrassed and was clearly torn between his conflicting loyalties. Wendy lived with him but Jo was his daughter. He turned to Gordy.

'I'll find my wife's address for you.'

Mark was the fourth member of the household to call on the landlord and he hoped that he would have more success than his friends. Karlene went with him to show him the way.

'Do you think it might work?' she said.

'Keep your fingers crossed.'

'I can't have my room in that state much longer.'

'You have to, for the time being. I know you want to clean it up but it's important that Mr Foss sees the full extent of the damage. What we won't tell him, of course, is that Bella brought down half the ceiling.' He smiled at the memory.

'Only because it was wet through.'

'Yes,' said Mark. 'If we didn't have that hole in the roof, she wouldn't have been up there at all. One thing led to another. Mr Foss is facing a much bigger bill now than he need have done.'

'Will he pay it, though?'

'Reg Beazely seems to think so. He said we had to force the landlord's hand.'

When Foss's house came in sight, Karlene stopped. 'You go on your own,' she told him. 'I'll wait here. Remember, Mr Foss warned me never to call on him again.'

'So what?'

'We don't want to antagonise him.'

'That's exactly what we do want to do, Karlene. It's the only language he understands, according to Mr Beazley. You're coming with me. It'll show him we mean business.'

'You're right, Mark. Let's go!'

They turned boldly into the drive and walked past the shiny Mercedes. When Foss answered the door, he noticed Karlene first.

'I thought I told you to stay away from here!' he growled.

'We came to deliver an ultimatum,' she said. Mr Foss grunted.

'A final demand,' said Mark, politely. 'I'm Mark Andrews and I'm one of the tenants in your house, too. Since you won't come to see the damage to your property, we've brought you a detailed list of everything that needs repairing.' He took out a long envelope. 'We got a builder to give us an estimate.'

'You can't do that!' snarled Foss.

'We can and we did.' Mark handed over the envelope. 'Read that and you'll see how serious the situation is.'

'I won't even open it.'

'In that case,' announced Karlene, 'we'll move out.'

'That suits me fine.'

'Tomorrow.'

'Without paying this month's rent,' added Mark. 'And don't think you'll be able to get new tenants in there. When they see the state it's in, nobody will touch that house. You'll have to spend money on repairs first.'

'We can't stand it any longer,' said Karlene.

'We're leaving tomorrow.'

'You're supposed to give a month's notice!' he argued, trapped. 'In writing. It's in the rental agreement.'

'You don't abide by it,' said Mark. 'Why should we?'

'You can't threaten me like this!' he shouted.

'Oh, I don't see why not,' said Karlene.

'Now don't take that tone with me, young lady.'

They had him worried now and Mark sensed it. He played his last card.

'Read that estimate, Mr Foss,' he said. 'The builder was disgusted with the state of the property. He said that any landlord should be ashamed to neglect a house so badly. You can have our keys back tomorrow.'

The two friends turned abruptly and walked away.

Suzie left the hospital by the exit where she was mugged. She hung about for several minutes, hoping she might see her attacker again. She and Tom seemed to be friends again but the only real way they could make it up was for her to get the demo tape back. In her heart, she knew it was unlikely, but she was still obsessed with scanning every face she saw, hoping she might recognise the guy who'd stolen it from her.

But the only face she recognised was Yvonne's.

'Hi, Suzie.'

'Oh, hello Yvonne.'

'How are you feeling now?'

'Bearing up.'

'Gordy told us you'd been mugged.'

'Yes,' she said. 'Only a short distance from where we're standing. He came out of nowhere and grabbed my bag.'

'Don't you carry a scream-alarm?'

'No. I can scream loud enough myself.'

'You should get one of these,' said Yvonne, taking a small buzzer from her pocket. 'Press this and it makes a horrendous noise. Enough to scare off most muggers, anyway.'

'I wish I'd had one then,' said Suzie, looking at it. 'But enough about me. How's Jo?'

'Much better today.'

'That's great.'

'Those tranquillisers seem to be working. Jo's much more relaxed and her memory's definitely coming back, slowly. Kim and I are taking it in turns to be with her. But Gordy's the real hero.'

'He really wants to help.'

'Well he's been fantastic,' said Yvonne, fondly. 'It's made me look at him in a new light. I always thought he was just out for a good time – someone who liked to chat up the girls.'

'There's a lot more to Gordy than that.'

'I know now. Who else would go all the way to Birmingham just to try and help a friend?'

'I think he feels responsible.'

'She's definitely on the mend.' Yvonne shook her head. 'Of course, she won't recover completely until we find out what's really causing her psychological pain.'

'That's what Gordy's gone to find out, hasn't he?'

'He's been fantastic.'

'You should tell him,' said Suzie, smiling. 'He'd love to hear you say that, Yvonne.'

The likeness was extraordinary. Doreen Barnes was an older version of her daughter. She had the same figure, the same features and the same hair. Under other circumstances, Gordy felt, she would have Jo's friendly smile.

'Where is she now?' asked Mrs Barnes.

'She's at her flat with Yvonne and Kim, her flatmates. They're keeping an eye on her – looking after her.'

'They're nice girls. I've met them both.'

'I told them exactly what Damian told me. So don't worry,' said Gordy. 'The three of us will get Jo through this somehow.'

'I'm so grateful she's got friends like you!'

They were in a flat in Harborne near to the Junior School where Jo's mother was the headteacher. Mrs Barnes was shaken when she heard the news about her daughter. She wanted Gordy to tell her all the details. A despairing look crossed her face.

'My husband will have to be told,' she decided.

'I've already spoken to him, Mrs Barnes. It was he who gave me this address.'

'Yes, I see.'

'He was going to ring you himself but I insisted on speaking to you first. I thought you'd rather hear the news from me. I hope that was right.'

'That was very considerate of you.'

'Needless to say, Jo doesn't know I'm here.'

'Of course not.'

'I didn't want to tip her over again.'

Mrs Barnes nodded. She was clearly very distressed and Gordy felt deeply sorry for her. To hear that her daughter was unwell was bad enough, but she also had to cope with the idea that she might, in some way, be responsible for Jo's breakdown.

'Did you meet my husband at his surgery?' she asked.

'No, I went to the house.'

'Then you probably met... Wendy. Miss Browning.'

'Yes, she let me in.'

'Wendy Browning was a receptionist at the surgery,' she explained, quietly. 'My husband began to see private patients at home and Wendy worked there with him two days a week. They were often alone together. That's when it started.'

'You don't have to tell me this, Mrs Barnes.'

'It's the only way you'll understand what happened to Jo. She idolised her father. All she ever wanted to be was another "Doctor Barnes". Then this happened. It's only three weeks since I moved out of the house.'

'So the pressure's been building up in Jo since then?'

'She was shattered,' said Mrs Barnes. 'At first, she just refused to believe it. She was on the phone every day, begging me to make it up with her father. As if it was my fault.' Tears welled up in her eyes. 'Jo found it very hard to accept that her father was the guilty party.'

'It's obviously been very upsetting for her.'

'And she never mentioned it to anyone?'

'No one, Mrs Barnes. Not to me, or to Kim and Yvonne. That was the problem, apparently. Trying to bottle it up inside her and throwing herself into her work to escape.'

Mrs Barnes took out a handkerchief and wiped her eyes. 'I'm coming with you,' she decided. 'I need to see Jo. I'll drive you back this evening, if you like.'

'Do you think it might be better to wait a while?' he suggested.

'She needs me. I must see her as soon as possible. I'm her mother.'

'That might be the problem,' he said, gently. 'We've seen how devastated Jo was when you and your husband split up. If you go and see her without her knowing you're coming, it might only make the situation worse. Jo's in such a delicate state.'

'I must see her.'

'You will, Mrs Barnes. But there might be a better way of doing it. It won't be easy but it's worth a try.'

'I don't understand,' she said.

'What do you think hurt Jo the most?'

'The split between me and my husband.'

'Exactly. And if you turn up, alone, on her doorstep, you'll just be a reminder of that split. Do you understand?'

'Yes, Gordy, I suppose you might be right,' she sighed.

'Then there's only one solution. Let me ring Doctor Barnes.'

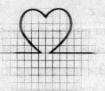

Chapter Sixteen

Bella was changing into her jeans and sweater when she heard the bumping. At first, she thought another bird had got into Karlene's room, but then she realised that the sounds were coming through the wall. She went out onto the landing and found Mark's door wide open. He was heaving a second suitcase down from the top of his wardrobe.

'What are you doing?' she said.

'Packing my bags, Bella.'

'But you're not going anywhere, are you?'

'No,' he said with a wink. 'But I'd better look as if I am. So had you. Suzie and Karlene have already done some of their packing. It's all for our dear landlord's benefit.'

'Do you think the bluff will work?'

'I hope so.'

'But supposing it doesn't? What will we do?'

'Then we really will have to find another place.'

'That won't be easy, Mark. Anyway, I don't want to move, I like it here.'

'Even with the moths and sparrows, Bella?'

'I'd stay here even if we had a bird sanctuary up in the loft,' she said, cheerfully. 'As long as the repairs are done, that is.'

'Well, it all depends on the estimate. If Mr Foss reads it, he's bound to take action. We're only students — he won't listen to us. But the chances are that because a professional builder tells him the house is a wreck, he won't be able to ignore us quite so easily.'

'It's ready!' called Suzie from the kitchen.

'Good,' said Bella. 'I'm starving.'

'So am I, but I daren't eat too much with the marathon only a few days away. The less weight I have to carry, the further I can run.'

They went down to the kitchen and found Karlene already sitting at the table. In spite of her broken fingers, Suzie had made a casserole, working patiently with one hand. Now she lifted the lid and the steam rose in a cloud. 'I made this as a thank you,' she said. 'You've all been so helpful since I was mugged.' Using oven gloves, Mark lifted the casserole onto the table and they were soon tucking into the food with relish.

'Delicious!' said Bella. 'By the way, Suzie, I saw something in the local paper that might interest you.'

'Oh? What was that?'

'Stress are playing again tomorrow night, in a pub in Bessemer Road – The White Lion, I think. I thought I'd warn you so that you can avoid it.'

'But I'm going to be at The White Lion tomorrow.'

'After what that rat, Tom, did to you?'

'We've made it up now. He came to the hospital at lunchtime to see me. I really want to go to the gig and Tom's given me a ticket.'

'Maybe I should come with you,' volunteered Mark. 'Bessemer Road is a rough area.'

'I'll be fine, thanks,' said Suzie. 'I went on my own before. Besides, Tom will bring me home in his van.'

'Tell him to park it right outside,' suggested Karlene. 'Then the five of us can sleep in the back – if the landlord doesn't give in, we'll be out on the street.'

They managed to laugh but it died quickly when they heard a loud banging on their door. Mark was the first on his feet. He looked through the window of the living room.

'Talk of the devil! He's here!'

'Old Fossie?' said Bella.

'As large as life and twice as nasty.'

'Let me deal with him,' said Karlene.

'No,' insisted Suzie. 'It's my job. And this time I'll try and do it properly.'

She went confidently to the front door and opened it wide. Alec Foss was about to say something when he saw the suitcases and bags stacked in the hall.

'You're serious, then, are you?' he said.

'We move into the new place tomorrow,' replied Suzie.

'New place?' He fingered his moustache. 'You got somewhere else, then?'

'For the time being. It's not as big as this house but at least we'll have a proper roof over our heads.'

'You've got one here!' he snapped.

'Give or take a few gaping holes.'

'It can't be that bad, Suzie,' he began to whine.

'Mr Beazely climbed up there to see for himself.'

'That's exactly what I've come to do,' said Foss. 'This estimate is ridiculous. I bet half the things on it aren't necessary. Reg Beazely's having me on.'

Suzie stood to one side. 'No he's not. Come and take a look.'

Foss thumped upstairs and they could hear him moving around heavily. When he climbed into the loft, they heard a howl as he banged his head. They tried desperately not to laugh.

'Serves him right!' spluttered Karlene.

'I hope he gets attacked by birds as well,' said Bella.

It was almost twenty minutes before Mr Foss reappeared. His suit was covered in white blotches and his bald head had a thin film of plaster dust on it.

He took out the estimate which Mark had given him and tore it up in front of them. For a moment, they were afraid they'd lost. But the landlord was no fool. He knew that they were good tenants. They always paid the rent on time and kept the house spotless. He would be unlikely to find any tenants as amenable as they had been.

'All right,' he growled, giving in at last. 'You'll get it done. But not by Reg Beazley. I'm not having him inside any of my properties. My own builder will be round later this evening to throw a tarpaulin over that roof.'

'We need more than that,' warned Suzie.

'First thing tomorrow, he'll be on site to mend the roof and replaster that ceiling. Now, are you going to stay?'

'If we're satisfied with the repairs,' said Suzie.

'Oh, you will be, don't you fret.'

With that, he left. As soon as they heard his car drive away, they clustered eagerly round Suzie.

'You were great,' said Bella.

'That bit about having somewhere to go really worried him,' said Karlene.

'Not as much as it scared me,' admitted Suzie. 'I was bluffing the whole time.'

Gordy was delighted by Jo's obvious improvement.

When he arrived at the flat, she was laughing at a sitcom on television. For a moment, Jo was back to her former, happy self.

'Hello, Gordy!' she welcomed. 'We were just talking about you.'

'No wonder my ears were burning.'

'Yvonne was saying some nice things about you.'

He glanced at Yvonne and saw her friendly smile. Jo switched off the TV.

'Where've you been all day?' she asked him.

'Oh, uh… out and about.'

'I was waiting for you to call. I thought you might come round earlier. Then you could have met him.'

'Who?'

'My other visitor,' said Jo, happily. 'Doctor Holt. He came this morning when I was here with Kim. He's really nice and it was kind of him to come in his free time. You'd really have liked him.'

Jo had clearly forgotten that Gordy already knew Damian, but he didn't correct her. Seeing her in such a bubbly mood was a tonic in itself.

'What did Doctor Holt say?'

'That I seemed much better.'

'Did he suggest anything else?'

'Yes, lots of time with my friends and get as much sleep and relaxation as I can.'

'We're here,' said Yvonne. 'You can call on us whenever you want.'

'Yes,' agreed Gordy. 'That's what we're here for.'

While Yvonne made them all coffee, he sat down to talk to Jo. Her physical improvement seemed to be matched by an improvement in her memory. Much more detail had come flooding back into her mind. There were still gaps, but she no longer felt adrift in a vacuum.

The three of them drank their coffee and chatted easily. When Gordy felt that Jo was truly relaxed, he strolled casually to the window. It was a signal to someone in a car outside. He turned to face Jo again.

'You look fantastic!'

'That's more than you do, Gordy. You look exhausted.'

'It's been a long, hard day.'

'Have you been revising?'

'In a way,' he said, looking rather nervous.

'I'm going to miss it,' she said, easily. 'I'm lucky. Doctor Holt has managed to explain to the hospital that I shouldn't sit the exam right now. I bet you envy me, Gordy.'

'I wonder if there's any chance of Damian getting me out of it, too?' mused Gordy.

Jo smiled. Just then there was a soft tap on the door.

'I wonder if that's your friend Doctor Holt again? Right on cue,' said Jo.

'No,' said Gordy, crossing to open the door. 'You've

got some other visitors this time, Jo.'

He let Doctor Barnes and his wife into the room. Jo stared at them in disbelief. Her father smiled at her and her mother held out both arms. There was a tense pause. Then, with tears streaming down her face, Jo ran towards them.

As both parents embraced their daughter, Gordy nodded to Yvonne and they both slipped quietly out of the room. They weren't needed now.

'I think Gordy deserves a medal,' said Mark.

'Yes,' agreed Suzie, 'but Yvonne might offer him something much nicer. She and Gordy have been thrown together by all this. By helping Jo, they were helping themselves as well.'

'Is Yvonne going out with him?'

'No, but they're revising for the exam together. That comes first. The rest will have to wait.'

'At least they won't have to worry so much about Jo.'

'No. She's gone home with her parents, Mark. Not that Jo's quite back to normal yet. There's still a long way to go. But Gordy's idea of bringing them in together seemed to work. Even if it was only a temporary solution. Doctor Barnes and his wife are still living apart. They only came down here together for Jo's sake.'

'Maybe they've learnt something from this?'

'We'll see,' said Mark. 'The main thing is that Jo's on the mend. She's going to stay with her mother in Birmingham and her father will pop across to see her every day.'

It was the end of the afternoon. They were sitting in the waiting room of the Outpatients' Department. Suzie had an appointment there so that her injured hand could be examined. Mark was keeping her company.

'Things are looking up all round,' he observed. 'You and Tom are friends again, Karlene will soon be back in her room and now there's real hope for Jo.'

'Win that marathon tomorrow and it'll have been an amazing week for all of us.'

'All I can guarantee is that I'll finish,' he said, pushing his glasses up the bridge of his nose. 'It doesn't matter if I come in first or last – I'll still make the money for the scanner.'

'We'll be there to cheer you on, Mark.'

'Blur and Boyzone and Oasis will do that. Those are the tapes I'll use during the race, on my Walkman. I run much better when I keep to a rhythm. A marathon can get very boring. You need something to listen to along the way.' He grinned at her. 'Pity that Stress tape went missing. Their music would've been perfect.'

Suzie suddenly stiffened. They were sitting with

their backs against the wall and her gaze had been drifting to and fro across the room. A newcomer attracted her attention. He looked around, then chose a seat beside an old woman with a large bag at her feet. Taking out a newspaper, he began to read but Suzie was certain that he was looking into her bag. Suzie was also sure that she'd seen him somewhere before.

He was a tall, thin guy with a gaunt face. He'd changed his hair and his clothes since she last saw him, but she remembered those angry eyes. And she'd felt the strength of his fist. Sure of what she saw now, she leapt up and pointed with her free hand.

'That's him!' she yelled. 'That's the thief who took my bag!'

The young man took one look at her then jumped up. Mark responded even more quickly. He darted across to the main exit to block off his escape. Suzie's cries had alerted a uniformed security guard who came in from another door. The mugger made a run for it, pulling a knife from his belt as he did so and swearing aloud.

As the security man tried to catch him, he slashed at him with the knife and opened up a deep gash in his sleeve. Blood oozed out and the guard clutched at his arm. Mark followed the young man as he went through the double doors and he saw him vanishing round a corner. He was fast but Mark had two advantages; his training schedule had made him very fit and he knew the hospital like the back of his hand.

As the mugger dived through another door, Mark knew exactly where he would come out and he took a short cut through the kitchens. The kitchen staff weren't pleased when a student nurse went sprinting past them knocking over a rack of saucepans, but Mark couldn't stop to explain. Catching the thief was the priority.

They came out into the corridor at exactly the same time as each other. The mugger slashed at Mark with the knife but he jumped back out of reach. When the attacker ran off again, Mark followed. The injured security guard had alerted his colleagues and two of them appeared at the far end of the corridor. Now that exit was cut off, the thief began to run up the main staircase. Mark slowly closed on him. He could hear him panting for breath as he struggled up the stairs.

When they reached the fourth floor, the youth tried a dash along a corridor but more security men were coming towards him and he was forced to make a run through one of the wards. The alarmed patients sat up in their beds when they saw a young man brandishing a knife. The nurses jumped out of the way and a woman pushing a trolley of magazines screamed in fear.

Mark saw his chance at last. If the man was

cornered, he would turn and attack with his knife. He had to be taken from behind, and now. Putting in an extra spurt, Mark flung himself forward, tackling him around the legs. He hit the floor with a hard thud and the knife was knocked out of his hand. This was the person who had grabbed Suzie's bag and broken her fingers, causing her all that distress and pain. When he tried to roll free, Mark showed him no mercy.

Sitting astride his chest, he punched him hard in the face and blood was soon streaming from the man's nose. By the time the security men arrived to help Mark, the thief was crying out to him to stop. Now Suzie had made her way up to the ward and confronted her attacker.

'That's him, that's the mugger who took my bag, for sure. Where's my tape?' she demanded. 'I want it back, now!'

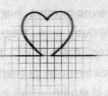

Epilogue

A large crowd turned out to watch the sponsored marathon. It was a fun event with a serious purpose. Most of the runners were wearing fancy dress and one even disguised himself as a nanny so that he could push an inflatable Santa Claus along in a big pram. Gordy, Suzie, Karlene and Bella stood near the finishing line, urging the competitors over the last few metres. Everyone who took part was earning vital money for the purchase of a new scanner for the hospital.

'No sign of Mark yet,' said Bella, searching the faces in the sea of runners coming towards her. 'Yesterday's heroics may have taken it out of him.'

'He's as fit as a fiddle,' said Karlene. 'Mark will be here soon. He may not win but he deserves a special prize.'

'For what, Kar?' asked Gordy.

'Catching that thief yesterday.'

'Mark was really brave,' said Suzie.

'He did the hospital a huge favour, too,' said Karlene. 'The youth who mugged Suzie had been taking things from the patients and staff for months. When the police went to his digs, it was packed with all the things he'd stolen.'

'Including the Stress tape!' reminded Suzie. 'We've got it back at last. Tom was really pleased with me but Mark deserves the credit. We made a copy of the tape and Mark's listening to it right now as he's running.'

'No wonder he hasn't arrived yet!' joked Gordy.

'Stress are great. You should listen to them yourself.'

'No, thanks, Suze. I've had enough of my own stress recently. I hadn't realised how much it had taken out of me. I'm exhausted. I feel as though I didn't manage to cure Jo's stress, I just absorbed it into my own body.' He grinned broadly. 'But there are compensations, and here's the main one.'

'Hi, Gordy,' said Yvonne as she joined them.

She said hello to the others then stood beside Gordy. He slipped an arm around her shoulders.

'Any word from Jo?' asked Karlene.

'Yes,' said Yvonne. 'She rang this morning.'

'How is she?'

'Over the worst. She doesn't fool herself that her parents are going to get back together just to please her, but at least she's talking to both of them again.

Her memory's filtering back now, too.'

'She's remembered the most important thing,' said Gordy.

'What's that?' asked Bella. 'Crashing your car?'

'Yes! It's really good news.'

'What's good about having your Astra in pieces?'

'I won't have to pay for the damage, Bel. Jo remembered that she's insured to drive any car. As she was behind the wheel, her insurance company will pay the costs. I rang the garage this morning with the good news.'

'Every cloud has a silver lining,' remarked Yvonne. 'As for Jo, she just needs time to recharge her batteries. Her mother will look after her and her father will be able to give any medical advice. We'll see her back before long, I'm sure. And by then, she'll have adjusted properly to the situation between her parents.'

Gordy laughed. 'All's well that ends well!'

'Talking of ending well,' said Suzie, 'here's Mark!'

'Come on!' urged Bella. 'Go for it, Mark.'

Suzie, Karlene and Yvonne started to chant, 'Come on Mark!' but Gordy stepped out onto the track and waved his arms at his friend.

'Stop!' he yelled. 'Fall over, Mark. Break a leg. Have a migraine. Lose your sense of direction. STOP!'

Bella and Karlene pulled him quickly out of the way.

'What are you doing?' they chorused.

'I owe him a small fortune if he gets to that tape.'

'Then get your wallet out,' said Yvonne, grinning. 'He's going to make it. On, on, on!'

Mark was running slowly and looked desperately tired but his determination took him over the finishing line. The four girls whooped with pleasure. Gordy groaned in mock horror and tried to work out how much he'd have to pay. The five of them pushed their way through the crowd until they reached Mark. Bending over with his hands on his knees, he was panting hard. He looked up at his friends with a brave smile.

'Are you OK?' asked Karlene.

'Chasing thieves is easier,' he said. 'They don't run for twenty-six miles.'

'I wish you hadn't!' said Gordy.

'All I can think about now is a hot bath.'

'I cleaned the bathroom specially for you,' said Karlene. 'And you won't have to lie in it and listen to moths and birds flying about in the loft. The slates are up and so is my ceiling.'

'Everybody's happy, then!' breathed Mark.

'Except me,' murmured Gordy.

'Don't be so mean!' said Yvonne, giving him a friendly dig in the ribs.

'Well, I suppose it's a good cause,' he said with a grin. 'I'll pay up. Now that I haven't got a garage bill to worry about, I can actually afford it.'

Suzie put a towel around Mark's shoulders and when he put out an arm for support, Bella and Karlene were there, too. The three girls were very proud of him.

'How was the Stress tape?' asked Suzie.

'Great! It really kept me going.'

'Tom's bound to ask me when I see him tonight.'

'Tell him that it ruined Mark's chances of winning,' said Bella. 'The music sent him to sleep.'

'If only it had!' mused Gordy.

'Tell him the songs were inspirational,' said Karlene.

'No,' added Mark between gasps. 'Tell Tom the truth. Stress took all the stress out of the race.'

They all laughed happily as they helped Mark home.

Order Form

To order direct from the publishers, just make a list of the titles you want and fill in the form below:

Name

....

Address

....

....

....

Send to: Dept 6, HarperCollins Publishers Ltd, Westerhill Road, Bishopbriggs, Glasgow G64 2QT.

Please enclose a cheque or postal order to the value of the cover price, plus:

UK & BFPO: Add £1.00 for the first book, and 25p per copy for each additional book ordered.

Overseas and Eire: Add £2.95 service charge. Books will be sent by surface mail but quotes for airmail despatch will be given on request.

A 24-hour telephone ordering service is available to holders of Visa, MasterCard, Amex or Switch cards on 0141-772 2281.

Collins
An *Imprint of* HarperCollins*Publishers*